Getting There

Published by Merlyn's Pen, Inc.
4 King Street
P.O. Box 1058
East Greenwich, Rhode Island 02818-0964

Printed in the United States of America.

These are works of fiction. All characters and events portrayed in this book are fictional, and any resemblance to real people or incidents is purely coincidental.

Cover design by Alan Greco Design.
Cover illustration by Christine Sivo. Copyright ©1986.
Section illustrations by Jane O'Conor. Copyright ©1995.

Library of Congress Cataloging-in-Publication Data

Getting there : seventh grade writers on life, school, and the
  universe / edited by Kathryn Kulpa.
        p.   cm. -- (American teen writer series)
    "All of the short stories in this book originally appeared in
  Merlyn's Pen: The national magazines of student writing"-
  -Acknowledgments.
    Summary: A collection of short fiction and non-fiction written by
  seventh-grade students, arranged under the headings "Around the
  Block," "Close to Home," and "Out of This World."
    ISBN 1-886427-04-6
    1. Children's Literature. 2. Children's writings, American.
  [1. Literature--Collections. 2. Children's writings.] I. Kulpa,
  Kathryn. II. Series.
  PZ5.G326   1995
  810.8' 09282--dc20   95-20070
                                                      CIP
                                                      AC

99 98 97 96   6 5 4 3 2

Getting There

SEVENTH GRADE WRITERS ON LIFE,
SCHOOL, AND THE UNIVERSE

Edited by
Kathryn Kulpa

The American Teen Writer Series
Editor: R. James Stahl

Merlyn's Pen, Inc.
East Greenwich, Rhode Island

Acknowledgments

Jo-Ann Langseth, copy editor, and Christine Lord, managing editor, are gratefully acknowledged for their significant work in preparing these manuscripts for original publication in *Merlyn's Pen: The National Magazines of Student Writing.*

All of the short stories and essays in this book originally appeared in *Merlyn's Pen: The National Magazines of Student Writing.*

The American Teen Writer Series

Young adult literature. What does it mean to you?

Classic titles like *Lord of the Flies* or *Of Mice and Men*—books written by adults, for adult readers, that also are studied extensively in high schools?

Books written for teenagers by adult writers admired by teens—like Gary Paulsen, Norma Klein, Paul Zindel?

Shelves and shelves of popular paperbacks about perfect, untroubled, blemish-free kids?

Titles like *I Was a Teenage Vampire? Lunch Hour of the Living Dead?*

The term "young adult literature" is used to describe a range of exciting literature, but it has never accounted for the stories, poetry, and nonfiction actually written by young adults. African American literature is written by African Americans. Native American stories are penned by Native Americans. The Women's Literature aisle is stocked with books by women. Where are the young adult writers in young adult literature?

Teen authors tell their own stories in *Merlyn's Pen: The National Magazines of Student Writing.* Back in 1985 the magazine began giving young writers a place for their most compelling work. Seeds were planted. Now, the American Teen Writer Series brings us the bountiful, rich fruit of their labors.

Older readers might be tempted to speak of these authors as potential writers, the great talents of tomorrow. We say: Don't. Their talent is alive and present. Their work is here and now.

About the Author Profiles:

The editors of the American Teen Writer Series have decided to reprint the author profiles as they appeared in *Merlyn's Pen* when the authors' works were first published. Our purpose is to reflect the writers' school backgrounds and interests at the time they wrote these stories.

Contents

Around the Block

Close to Home

Out of this World

Around the Block

He's a smooth operator . . .

Weston Library

by ANDREW NOZIK

T here I was, sitting with my pals in the corner of the library, all of us holding some books that we had picked up from the shelves so we could look busy. I was starting a report about King Arthur and his Knights of the Round Table when she walked in. The sunlight glimmered off her shiny brown hair. I thought to myself that she couldn't be from Weston. She was way too pretty. The way she glanced around, studying every little minute detail of the front hall, gave away that she hadn't been here before. She almost bumped into the card catalog in the center of the room. I always thought it was a silly place for it.

"Yo, guys, look who just walked in." My voice, low and solid, came out leisurely and forced them to look. Why I always tell them everything is beyond me. Three years, I've told them everything; why'd I tell them this? They all looked. She gracefully turned from the card catalog, looked in our direction, and smiled. Her moist lips tightened as the skin stretched back into a small semicircle. I thought my eyes were playing tricks on me, fooling me into thinking that she was prettier than she really was. My left thumb itched with anticipation. OK, keep cool. Relax. Nothing embarrassing will happen. Just stay cool.

She started to walk over to us. Her hips swayed from side to side. You could tell something was going to happen. She had deep, dark brown eyes that matched her hair. Beauty was almost near. My group started acting like wild boars, and one almost grunted. Ace even went so far as to whistle at her.

She came up to the table, looked around, and sat in an empty chair next to mine. She looked at me with a peculiar expression. Our eyes met. Mine flashed back to the herd. Each one of them was staring right back at me. I looked at her again. No one said anything. As always, I was the one who started things up.

I could see now that the skin on her face was smooth, soft, and silky. I could smell her perfume drifting over the piles of books between us on the table and lingering in the space in front of me. By now my thumb throbbed in pain, as I had all I could do to keep from scratching it.

The tension in our corner of the room felt as if it would explode. Alex had laid down his book and just sat there open-mouthed, staring at her. Beauty kept her cool. I could tell she had dealt with situations like this before. It seemed as if the whole library had dropped what it was doing and was looking at us. Ted shrank back in his seat and became smaller. The herd was whimpering. They fell to her power, as they had to mine. If the bus hadn't come so early this morning, I might have had time to rehearse my well-known lines of "What ya doin' after school today?" or "Do you want to go to the Center?"

Tom almost bowed to her as if he were her personal slave, and Jake was close to yelping in horror as her gaze pierced through him. They googooed as she flicked her brown hair with her delicate hand. The raising of my right eyebrow at her, however, pushed them back into their seats and kept them there. Sam dropped his book on medieval knights and totally forgot about his research paper, which was already late. Beauty and I seemed to share this power over people. I don't know if it made us superior or if they were simply weaker, but either way I liked it.

Beauty was relaxing by leaning back and letting the two front legs of her chair lift off the floor. But wait a minute . . . why is she looking at Tom? Doesn't she know that he is the stupidest one here? Look at that dumb look on his face. He can't even do an addition problem without a calculator. She might consider Freddie if he would open his mouth and say something. Or Jack might win her hand if he wouldn't fool around so much and actually think.

But not to worry—I was King! I knew all of them better than they knew themselves, could anticipate their every move. Yes, I had mastered them. And she knew it. She turned back to me. King Arthur and his Queen were on their thrones; peasants would have to beg for mercy! The library was our castle, and Weston our kingdom.

ABOUT THE AUTHOR

Andrew Nozik lives in Weston, Massachusetts, where he attends Weston Middle School. Among his interests are reading, computers, photography, coin collecting, and woodworking. Favorite sports include swimming, kayaking, snorkeling/scuba diving, baseball, and wrestling.

She has to be good at *something*!

The Great Talent Search

by Janani Krishnaswami

Meet the one and only Andrea Harlow, Girl Who Shows No Potential Talent for Anything. Yep, you heard me—or rather, read me—right. I show absolutely no budding talent for anything at all. I do try, y'know, but things just never seem to work out, so here I am, stranded and alone, with no talent to call my own. All those child prodigy kids—you know, the kind who take ballet lessons on Sundays, flute lessons on Mondays, piano on Tuesdays, tennis on Wednesdays, and art classes on Fridays—they're probably doubled over on the ground right now, crying, "No more! Please! Stop torturing me!" Indeed, I thought I should place a warning sign on this essay: "All children who have heart trouble, are hypertensive, or are asthmatic should consult their physician before attempting to read the following paragraphs." But I decided people would decide for themselves whether they wanted to read this or not. So, since you're probably going to read this no matter what I say, I guess I should begin at that weird day they call "the first day of school."

English teachers wouldn't be English teachers if they didn't assign some sort of essay sooner or later. Well, it happened, though a little earlier than expected. "What do you think is inside the real you?" was the task this time. I wrote on and on about little green men with antennae, entering my body, walking through my veins, and riding a boat along my bloodstream, all the while taking notes on a small pad. After they feasted on my food, they started to chant: "Give up, give up, it isn't worth it!" until my whole insides were brainwashed into chanting, "Give up, give up . . ." Shoot, I even threw in a little harmony—the green guys altos and my body the soprano. Finally, the greens took a box marked 'Potential Talents' from a group of boxes next to my heart and flew away in their UFO. Proudly, the next day, I handed in three pages filled with my scrawly handwriting. Miss Andrews skimmed the first couple of paragraphs and looked at me as if I had a cabbage for a head. Needless to say, I ended up having to write it again. Hey, what can you do when teachers are too dense to appreciate great talent?

Then, the poetry assignment. Hesitant, I sat down at our computer and began typing. When the dust cleared, I saw that (to my surprise) a poem was actually sitting there on the screen, with—lo and behold!—a title as well! And it was titled (drum roll, please) "Suicide." I stared at it and read it. Then I gave a yelp of surprise. It was an honest-to-goodness poem! It actually did all the things poems are supposed to do! Unfortunately, my mother just happened to be wandering by, and she was so surprised I had written a poem that she put a cold cloth on my forehead and gave me aspirin, despite my protests. Then she read it. I don't know how it happened, but we ended up sobbing in each other's arms. That night we had a Family Discussion on Why Suicide Is Not the Answer. Oh well, throw that one out the window.

I decided to give up on English and anything connected to it, and go on to real "art"—the drawing kind. After all, it seemed easy enough: a few straight lines here and there, some squiggly curlicues, and *voilá*—a picture! My first attempt (shall we call it heroic effort?) was a picture of a typical scene from our town. I started working at four that afternoon.

At ten o'clock, I proudly showed it to my parents, who looked at each other as if to say, "OK, who's going to smooth things with Andrea?" My father started biting his nails, looking really embarrassed. He stared pointedly at my mother, who then started shuffling around, chewing on her hair. She stared at my father pleadingly. My father looked around desperately and grabbed the telephone as if it were an oasis in a desert. My mother looked daggers at him. I, meanwhile, was not enjoying the drama. "Well?" I asked impatiently.

My mother looked desperately at my father, who was talking on the phone. He looked very guilty, but did nothing. My mother hesitated, then said encouragingly, "That's a very nice picture of . . . of . . . a . . . girl walking, ah, two dogs outside a, ah, row of houses, Andrea. And that hydrant next to the dogs looks so, ah, inviting—to the dogs, that is! But what I can't un-

derstand is why the balloon that little girl is holding
is so bumpy . . ." Well. We have to say my mother
tried. I guess she couldn't have known it was a picture
of a boy chasing three dogs away with a stick, and that
the scenery was two tall apartment buildings with grocery stores.

The violin, so sweet to everyone's ears! I decided
to take *that* up. But then my parents started making
mystery visits to the dentist, neighbors, grocery stores—
and wouldn't you know it, just when I was practicing. One day they came back from a long walk, and
they looked absolutely bushed. Mud and sweat coated
their bodies. Their first words were, "Andrea, did you
finish practicing?" When I said no, I think my mother
fainted dead away in my dad's arms. It was hard to
tell because at that moment my dad put his arms around
her for support.

Finally, when my teacher declared that she had some
unexpected family business to take care of, and that,
sadly, she couldn't teach anymore, I got really suspicious. Of course, I wasn't surprised when I saw that
same teacher teaching another violin student at the
same time the following week. I sidled up to her and
noted, "Family business over pretty quick, huh?" She
whirled around and looked very sheepish.

That gone too, I turned to photography. I obtained
my dad's camera and snapped pictures of everything
in sight. I photographed a still life of my younger sister's food—three scrambled eggs with a mound of sugar
on top, decorated by rivulets and valleys of jelly, a few
slabs of butter surrounding the foot of the structure,
a fake wax cherry stuck on top, and a fork stuck halfway
through the . . . uh . . . creation. I even managed to cap-

ture my sister's face as she took her first bite. Then I also photographed my older sister sleeping with her bottom sticking up in the air and drool pouring (and when I say pouring, I mean *pouring*) out of her mouth. I think my family was relieved when the roll of film was finished, though I really can't guess why.

Then I started developing them myself, feeling very proud. So proud, in fact, that I called up my best friend to tell her about my new hobby—whereupon Sarah went into major hysterics, shrieking, "A photographer? A PHOTOGRAPHER? Yeah, right, Andrea! I'll bet the last time you held a camera was in second grade. Remember? You snapped a picture and it blew up right in your face!"

I replied, "It did *not* blow up in my face, Sarah! I simply pressed the button that closes the lens instead of the one that takes the picture, and somehow the lens closed on my finger, and I started hopping around, and by accident I pressed the button that opens up the back of the camera, and the camera opened, and the exposed film fell out and scrunched real hard against my sore finger, so then I dropped the camera onto the sand, and my sister stepped on it by accident, and that's when it gave a little . . . uh . . . *boom*, or whatever—that's all!"

"That's all?" Sarah snorted. But by then, I remembered my pictures and rushed to them. Too late. They were all overdeveloped. Thanks a bunch, best friend.

Then I felt them, the Psychic Powers, whispering: *P. E.! P. E.!* The perfect solution. Be an athlete! Try volleyball! So there I stood at the front of the net, ready to spike the ball and send it whamming through the floor so hard there'd be smoke pouring out and it'd take the fire department to pull it, smoldering, from the ground. I readied myself, arms in position, an ever-so-slight crouch to my body, teeth gritted, sunglasses positioned an oh-so-subtle nudge down the nose, hair pulled neatly back into a braid.

"Zero all!" Sarah called. She whacked that ball straight across the net. I could see the white sphere, hurtling through the air, gleaming white, shining, waiting for my slam. I stared at it in wonder, watching the sun reflect off its whiteness. I could feel the tension around me. I could hear the cries of "Hit the ball, Andrea, hit the ball!" And I heard the thump of the ball as it hit the ground. I stared at the white sphere, entranced. And then I heard mumbles of "Andrea, it was right to you!" and "Andrea, how come you didn't hit the ball?" and "Jeez, Andrea, pay attention!" Yep, and when I recovered, I knew that the score was "one serving zero," and that volleyball was definitely not my sport.

Finally, one day I woke up and thought, *Life is a stinking, smelly cesspool filled with dirty people with dirty feet, overflowing with dirty comments with dirty meanings and dirty test papers (anything less than a B- is dirty to me) and . . .* By the time I got the courage to go to school, I was a nervous wreck. I told my pal Sarah, "What's the use? I had hope for me, but now I wonder if I'm a total idiot."

She didn't look up from her test paper (clean, with an A+ on it), but my ears caught her muttering, "Took her long enough to figure it out!" I mean, talk about supportive best friends! I was so depressed that when I got home I sat down at my computer and began typing. This time, when the dust cleared, wonder of wonders, I saw—could it really be? Was it an optical illusion?—an essay! And, omigosh! It was actually good! I dared not show it to my mother for fear we would end up sobbing over the computer again.

Well! What the heck am I going to do with it? If I decide to take a chance—you only live once, or whatever the saying is—I'll see how it fares in the wonderful world of professional story writers and poets. Well, I don't have anything to lose, do I? Come to think of it, though, I have earned a solid reputation as a non-potentialistic (or whatever you call people with no creative potential) person, so if I do fare well, it just might ruin my one claim to fame! Do I want to risk that? I know, I know, you're probably staring at this and going, "Huh?" But hey! Take it from me—it's written in the stars that Lady Luck has to smile down upon me sometime. I mean, come on—have I ever been wrong?

ABOUT THE AUTHOR

Janani Krishnaswami lives in Jubail, Saudi Arabia, where she is a student at Jubail Academy. "Annoying people with my corny jokes, conquering the habit of chewing on my hair, and controlling my temper" are some of her daily intentions, along with "making people laugh and getting my little sister all riled up at least once a day." Pastimes include reading, writing, and "watching what is unfairly called the 'idiot box.'"

It was his chance to be a hero . . .

A Night in Lights

by F*RED* H*EYNE*

The best day of my life was actually the best night
of my life. It was the second baseball game of
our Tournament Team. I was one of the lucky
ones chosen to be on the Post Oak Little League Tournament Team. We had already won our first game, and
we were now playing Spring Branch American. The
pitcher for the other team threw his fastball around
55 miles per hour. The curve balls he threw were not
curving, and the changeups didn't change, but that
fastball was speedy and accurate. Throughout the game
the score inched up little by little. We were ahead; then
they were ahead. This went on until the last inning,
when they were up by one run. We were the home
team and would bat last.

Our first hitter came up to the plate and struck out
on three pitches. Our next batter crushed a double.
The crowd went crazy! The score, unfortunately, remained nine to eight, their lead. The next batter for

our team struck out within seconds. With the score
nine to eight and one man on base, guess who had to
bat next? I walked slowly up to the plate. My hands
were sweating so badly that the grip tape on the bat
became moist. Needing a kind word of encouragement, I looked over at my coach. "Come on, Fred.
Make a contribution to your team!" he said.

*Thanks, Coach. I can always count on you to in-
crease the pressure*, I thought to myself. I was actually
hoping for "You can do it, Fred!" or "We're all behind
you!" I stepped into the batter's box and spit. I fig-
ured if the pros do, why not? But since my mouth was
awfully dry, nothing came out, and I made sort of a
goofy noise. I looked at the pitcher. He was about 5'6",
black, and skinny. He wore his hat on the very top of
his head. He looked at me and sneered. Intimidation
is not a strong enough word to describe what that
pitcher was doing. I saw the umpire squat down and
motion for the pitcher to pitch the ball. *Oh, God, please
let me hit the ball. I don't care if it's a little dinker. Just
let me make contact with it,* I thought.

The first pitch came screaming in. *Whiff!* I swung
hard and missed. I can't really say what I thought at
that moment, but, believe me, it wasn't about church
and sunny days. The pitcher, now feeling extremely
studly, strutted back to the pitching rubber. I looked
down at my bat and a drop of sweat dripped off the
handle. My knees were wobbly from the pressure that
was chewing on my insides. The pitcher then wound
up, but in midmotion he slowed down. I knew the
pitch was a changeup, so I didn't swing. "Ball one!" I
could see he was a little ticked that I hadn't swung at
his sucker pitch. He looked at me and then walked

slowly back onto the mound. Then he wound up and threw a fastball. *Crack!* My heart did a triple gainer. I hit the ball. I couldn't believe it! But as I was rounding first base, I heard, "Foul ball!" My gainer had just turned into a belly flop.

I could have killed that umpire because now I had two strikes against me. The next pitch was in my happy zone, so I swung at it. *Crack!* Foul ball. After the fourth foul ball, every single person in the stands was a nervous wreck. My teammates shouted words of encouragement, but to me the shouts were just a constant hum filling my head. The pitcher was not too thrilled that after six pitches I was still at bat. So he decided to throw softly and get the ball over the plate for the third strike. As I saw the ball slowly coming toward me, I swung the bat while popping my hips and wrists at the same time. I had made contact with the ball! The sound the bat made at that moment was probably the prettiest noise I ever heard. I sprinted to first, and as I rounded the base, I saw the ball soaring high in the air. The ball traveled past the shortstop and was heading for the left fielder. He saw that it was going to be over his head, so he started running back toward the fence. As the ball cleared the left field wall, I could see him throwing his glove down on the ground.

I immediately went into a strange sort of shock. I was physically there, but mentally I was off in La-La Land. I could hear the fans screaming, but only faintly. When I touched home plate, the whole team came out and picked me up. I must have received one thousand high-fives and heard "I can't believe you hit a home run!" a million times. The pitcher went nuts and threw his glove in the trash can. He then ran into his own team's dugout and started trashing all of the equipment while crying and screaming uncontrollably. His coach had to tackle him to save all their expensive gear. I felt sorry for the guy, but somebody had to win. I'm not sorry that we were the ones.

I still have the ball in a case, and it warms me up like a cup of hot chocolate on a winter's night. I will always, even when I am one hundred years old, remember that night as the best night of my life.

ABOUT THE AUTHOR

Fred Heyne attends River Oaks Baptist School in his hometown of Houston, Texas. He enjoys hanging out with friends, playing his guitar and drums, and writing. Basketball, soccer, tennis, and running track are other favorite pastimes.

Machine vs. man: Who will win?

Computer Glitch

by BRIAN VEITH

Tuesday morning began badly. My digital watch overslept, throwing my whole schedule off-balance. Then, while I was trying to get a spoon and breakfast bowl from the dishwasher, the door bit my fingers. The microwave proceeded to convert my instant oatmeal into instant asphalt. This black, gooey stuff set off the smoke alarm. I finally had to remove the battery to stop its whine.

Later, in science class, events got decidedly worse. On Tuesday, Activity Day, students must work independently on projects. My chore was to load the data from my science fair project into the computer. At the end of the period, I was exhausted but satisfied that I had done a decent job of typing all those endless numbers. My eyes were bleary, my fingers cramped. Then it happened. I watched in anguish as my careful editing abruptly disappeared from the lighted screen. I searched frantically through the memory of the wretched machine, but no lost image appeared.

I did not want to contemplate my science teacher's grim reaction to my apparent lack of productivity. A hasty note of explanation ran from my brain to my nervous fingers. There was just enough time to type this memo and save it before the bell rang. During study hall, I returned to print it. Swiftly, I instructed the computer to save the message under "Computer Glitch." Immediately, disaster struck again. An eerie green streak flickered across the screen. The stubborn machine murmured a series of beeps and growls as if it were preparing to attack me. Without warning, the printer, which I had not even touched, began rolling paper out at my feet. I peered apprehensively at the monitor. The brief letter had vanished. I prudently reached for the OFF switch, resolving to compose a handwritten message at home that night.

That evening, I contemplated the computer's strange reaction. Perhaps it thought I was criticizing when I labeled the letter "Computer Glitch." No! Machines do not think! I located some notebook paper and reached for my pencil. The lead was too dull for legible writing. Leaning across my drafting table, I shoved the pencil into the electric sharpener. I should have known. The sharpener ate the entire thing. All that was left was the stub of lead surrounded by the metal band and the pink eraser. In my head, I could hear the mechanical gadgets laughing softly at me.

ABOUT THE AUTHOR

Brian Veith attends Fairfield Middle School in Fairfield, Ohio. His hobbies include soccer, playing the French horn, and model trains.

How do you say goodbye to a best friend?

Tawanda!

by CHRISSIE ANN GREEN

It was the last day. Could you believe it? No more sunny days at the pool or going to Jeffrey's and trying on ballroom dresses. Or funny sleepovers when we would wake up at midnight with a craving for homemade brownies with chocolate chips. It was all over.

See, Kristen was my best friend. She stood by me last February when my 72-year-old grandfather died of cancer. I can remember it so clearly. I was in the funeral parlor, crying. I had to go there three days in a row. No one was there for me. On the third day, I was in the hall trying to stop whimpering when the front door opened. She was there. She held my hand and talked about more cheerful and glorious things than death.

I can remember going to see movies at Roosevelt Field. I especially remember the movie *Fried Green Tomatoes*. Our favorite word was "tawanda," and it came from that movie. We said it when we tried to eat a lemon with sugar on top without squinting. We said it when we dove off the high dive for the first time. Or even just trying blueberry ice cream, we said it. It was the word of freedom to us. As if we we would always be like the Three Stooges doing stupid things.

But not anymore. She would never be there again. Because, just like my grandfather, she left too, though not in the same way.

She left in a truck with her family. She rode in a truck with furniture.

We walked into her house for the last time and saw that kitchen, with no refrigerator or microwave popping with popcorn, with no furniture in her den. We were surrounded by white walls in her room: empty, empty. I could visualize the two beds parallel to each other, one with Little Mermaid blankets and the other plain peach. I could see her little sister playing on the bed with the hamster and saying, "Chrissie, Chrissie, pick me up!" and hugging my legs because she was so short, and seeing that huge smile on her face when I gave her gum.

We left the house and I saw Kristen for what seemed like the last time, standing there in her black and orange Umbros, orange shirt, white Keds, and a narrow white headband. Turning her head and holding me with a grin, she said it—the one word that meant everything to us—"Tawanda!" She smiled and started to laugh. Then she climbed into the truck and said "Connecticut or Bust!"

ABOUT THE AUTHOR

Chrissie Ann Green lives in New Hyde Park, New York, and attends Herricks Middle School in Albertson, New York. She is active in sports as a member of her school's basketball and soccer teams. She also plays on a traveling soccer team, the New Hyde Park Wildcats. Other interests include music and dancing.

Will he choose friendship—or popularity?

The Ultimatum

by Kris Reich

The bell rang, interrupting my pleasant daydreams. John quickly hit me on the shoulder and told me that we were going to be late for the bus. I struggled out of my chair and ran for the door, which was filled with a mob of eighth-, ninth-, and tenth-graders. On our way to my locker I saw Erik. As soon as I spotted him, I looked at the floor.

"What a loser," John mumbled. Erik turned around in disgust.

John saw me looking at the ground. "What's the matter?" he asked.

"Nothing," I lied. Erik had always been a friend of mine, but times had changed. Now I wouldn't be caught dead with him in public.

With that, John and I proceeded to the bus. We sat in the back, where our gang was harassing a little fifth-grader. He started to cry, so we left him alone. Then we talked about losers in our grade. Erik was soon brought up in the conversation.

"Erik is such a fat loser," John said.

"Lay off Erik, you hardly know him."

"I think Peter may have the hots for Erik. Are you one of those types?" joked one member of the gang.

"Shut up!" I replied.

The gang and I did not talk for the rest of the bus ride. Soon John and the rest of the gang got off, and Erik and I were the only ones left. I moved to the front seat and sat down next to him.

"How's life?" I asked.

"None of your business."

"I know you must be a little mad, but I tried to stick up for you when they started harassing you."

The bus pulled to a screeching stop, and we got off.

"Some friend you are. You're embarrassed to speak to me in the halls for fear of wrecking your reputation. You're a stupid snob!"

Without thinking, I drew back my hand and swung hard at his nose. The blow sent him stumbling into the snowbank.

I looked at him and at the blood all over the snowbank. I gave a little chuckle, for form's sake, and ran toward my house.

I got to my driveway; I could already hear the screams from the house. My legs were tired, and I was breathing so hard it could be heard next door.

When I opened the door, the fighting ceased. My dad was the first to talk. "Oh, great. Our darling boy is here. He gives so much devotion and love to his parents. The minute he gets home he parades up to his room."

"I'm just sick of your fighting all the time."

"When I get through with you, you're going to wish you were never alive."

This time my mother cut in: "If you lay one hand on my boy, we're going to leave."

"You just stay out of this."

I waited until the fight was back in full swing and they didn't even know I was in the room. Then I slipped upstairs.

When I got to my room, I quickly turned on my radio to drown out the screams of the fight. I was getting used to the fighting, but it still made me sick to hear them.

I was up in my room thinking of excuses not to do my homework. Then I thought of the problem with Erik. He *was* a loser. If a loser had talked to John like that, John would have killed him.

Then my concentration was broken by a vigorous knock at my bedroom door. It was John. I invited him in.

"Do your parents always fight like this?"

"No, it just started a week ago when my dad was fired."

"I heard what you did to Erik."

"He deserved it. Why should I let him talk to me like that?"

"What I came over for is to ask you why you even talk to that scum Erik."

"I guess it's a change from being a loser to being popular." There was a bad crash of a chair downstairs, and I turned up my radio louder.

"You know, if you were to hit me or any other member of the gang, you would be in the hospital right now."

"Well, I didn't, so get off my case." I wanted to take back what I said, but he cut me off.

"You better watch how you talk to me." He left, and the door slammed hard behind him.

I couldn't understand John. Why didn't he hit me?

That night I lay in bed thinking over the bad things. I thought back to when I had gotten an F on my history test. I thought about my parents. Then the problem with Erik. Was it all right to hit him? Why didn't John hit me? If only I could take that back, I would have never hit Erik. Finally, I went to sleep.

I got up the next morning dreading the coming praise for hitting Erik, when praise wasn't necessary from my point of view. At 7:30 A.M. I headed for the bus. I saw Erik sitting in the front of the bus by himself. I had half a mind to stop and apologize, but John and the gang approached me.

"The gang and I were talking, and we decided that you have to choose—Erik or us! Because this could damage our reputation as well as *ruin* yours," said John.

I looked at Erik, then back at John.

The answer must have been written all over my face, because John reached out his hand and said, "Welcome back."

ABOUT THE AUTHOR

Kris Reich lives in Chagrin Falls, Ohio, and attends Hawken School in Lyndhurst. He enjoys sailing, tennis, skiing, and swimming.

Being homeless means
losing more than a place to live . . .

Invisible

by DOUG HABER

You on the street corner, night after night, day after day, sleeping and begging, the lowest of the poor. With your back carelessly laid against the cement wall of a building, waiting for money, waiting for someone, waiting for a time when you are no longer a nobody, not just another "bum," but rather a member of a community that accepts you. You think about what your life has been reduced to now that unemployment, poverty, and loneliness have taken over.

Many years ago you were living in an apartment, your income filtering steadily into your bank account. But then the blow came. The ring of a telephone awoke you, and as you answered the phone and listened, your eyes widened. Your hands started trembling, then wildly shaking. A frog crept into your throat as you heard the news. You, along with several others at the factory, had been fired. From there your life fell apart. Your rent was five months overdue, and you were kicked out of your apartment. You struggled for work, but there was none to be found. You tried at other factories but found that there, too, people had been laid off. You even tried at McDonald's, but they were only hiring friendly high school students, not older men. Now your home is the street.

Your clothes. They are dirty and dampened from the night's rain which poured down upon your defenseless body. Your eyes. They are softened and broken, as if beaten by the world entire. Your spirit, personality, and brilliance should not be confined to the body of a non-working man. You should be a brain surgeon or a senator. That spirit should be let out into the body of a free man, where your ingenuity could be used and appreciated. Your hands. They are wrinkled and blemished, with blue veins flowing around them. They are torn and bloodied from countless hours of rummaging through the steaming piles of garbage.

People walking by you look away, as if you are invisible. They refuse to acknowledge your humanity. They do not realize that you have emotions and a heart. When they see you pleading for a second chance at work, for a second chance at life, they look straight ahead, embarrassed by your presence.

At the day's end you look into your cup of nickels, dimes, and pennies and sigh heavily. It was not a good day. No day is good if you have no one who cares, no one who loves you. You drift off to sleep. Soon it will be nightfall, and all that can be distinguished is the misty outline of your tired, worn body.

There are hundreds of thousands of homeless men, women, and children living all over the streets in our country. You are one of these people. Every day you hope for work, going to the employment offices, but you know in the back of your mind that for the rest of your life you will be homeless. I am only twelve now, but when I have a job of my own I will help you, give you a job, or food, or just be someone to talk to. Maybe.

ABOUT THE AUTHOR

Doug Haber is a student at Weston Middle School in Weston, Massachusetts. He enjoys playing team sports, such as ice hockey, baseball, soccer, football, and basketball.

Coming in last doesn't mean being a loser!

The Pathetics

by MATTHEW BENNETT

The roar of the crowd throbs throughout the stadium—this batter could be the game's last. The Cleveland pitcher runs the count full 3-2. The pennant is on the line as the pitcher winds and delivers. The fastball sails over the heart of the plate, but the batter still misses the hurtling horsehide by several inches. The ball comes to rest in the catcher's mitt with a sizzling slap, and the Indians nip the Yankees and swipe the pennant.

This scene is from the movie *Major League*, where a baseball team grabs the pennant. But in my first Little League season, the only thing *we* grabbed was a bunch of dandelions in left field.

My team, the Athletics (more commonly known as the Pathetics by members of opposing teams), was cruising along at an 0-7 clip when we reached our last game. This stretch of futility included about five double-digit losses and one 28-0 thrashing. Our upcoming game against the Mets would make the difference between being called a bunch of losers by everybody, or only being called a bunch of losers by everybody but one team.

The first five innings were nothing short of miraculous. Our starting pitcher was phenomenal, giving up a mere five runs over five innings. Our hitting was even better—we scored six runs. It seemed like the Pathetics of old were transforming into the new and previously invisible Athletics.

We went down in order to the top of the sixth, which left us with just a one-run lead to defend going into the final inning of the game.

For the critical sixth inning, my coach gave me the chance to finish off the Mets. My hands were shaking; I had never pitched in a game that had less than a nine-run deficit and had never thrown after the third inning. Still, I managed to retire the first batter on a slow roller to first base.

The second batter, who could also make the possible tying run, singled down the third-base line.

After I struck the third batter out on four pitches, the crowd actually became raucous, unruly, and uncivilized. (Well, compared to a group of old ladies at bingo they were.) But that was still far rowdier than our fans had ever been. They were going insane like this in hopes of a Pathetics' first win of the year. With win number one (and only) on the line, I wound and delivered to the batter.

The pitch sailed over the plate and was greeted by the bat. The ball bounced to the shortstop, who, realizing that the runner would be forced out if he threw to second, did just that. The second baseman took the toss, stepped toward the base, and . . . dropped the ball.

Pandemonium broke out as the new Athletics re-verted to the Pathetics of old. At this point, my team-mates somehow managed to run into the ground, into the fence, and into each other. When the dust had cleared, both the batter and runner had scored, the ball came to rest wedged into the fence with a dull *thunk*, and the Athletics were 0-8.

The loss had struck so quickly and suddenly that we all stumbled back to our dugout in a daze. While we were sitting on the bench, stewing in our sweat and humiliation, somebody chuckled. This started every-body chuckling and shaking their heads. Maybe it was because we were so bad that it was funny, maybe it was happiness that the season was over, or maybe it was because we simply didn't have any other emotions left to use. Whatever the reason, the chuckles grew into a "we're number five" chant that echoed across the dusky, silent ballpark.

ABOUT THE AUTHOR

Matthew Bennett attends Hollis/Brookline Jr. High School in Hollis, New Hampshire. He writes: "As a 14-year-old baseball fan, I have been forced (by the strike) to watch endless reruns of Saturday Night Live. *This is OK because it's my favorite show."*

Finding the courage to stand against racism . . .

Cherokee

by KOREN ZIEMIENSKI

They're looking at me again. They always look at me. Then they giggle and turn away. I wish they wouldn't do that. I wish I hadn't moved. No one teased me where we used to live. We were all alike.

Now I'm different. Different from anyone else. My mother says I should be proud, but it's hard being proud when nineteen pairs of eyes are staring at you.

Once, a few even came over to my seat and called me a nigger. I have nothing against black people, but I am not one. I have dark skin and my hair is jet black, but I'm not black. I'm Indian. A pure Cherokee Indian and sometimes I wish I weren't. While my hair is black, theirs is brown and sometimes yellow. My skin is the color of light toast; theirs is like milk or cream.

I do not know why all the popular girls have yellow hair and milk-white complexions and pretty, full lips. They giggle a lot and bat their eyelashes at the boys. If only the boys knew what was under the smiles and giggles of some of those eyelash-batters.

All the girls wear those plastic bracelets that click when they walk, but I wear the beaded bracelet I made myself. It took me hours, for I dropped a great many beads and had to hunt for them in the cracked linoleum of our kitchen floor.

After school I walk home and sit in my kitchen with a little brother or two in my lap. I talk to my mother while she makes our supper. Later my father comes home and sweeps all of my little brothers into his great arms at once. They squirm and laugh. Then he leans over and kisses my cheek. He puts my brothers down and gives my mother a hug, and her black eyes dance like two mischievous shiny buttons. Then we all sit down to supper, and Haim, my littlest brother, puts margarine on his nose.

The next day, in school, the teacher says she has a surprise for us. Some kids groan and make catcalls, and others giggle. After they have quieted down, the teacher ushers in an Indian girl. She is silent and serious, but her eyes dart about the room. The teacher says that her name is Carlota. Her hair is jet black, not unlike mine, and hangs straight down her back to her waist. She wears a regular-looking blouse and a green skirt. Her eyes are as shiny as my mother's, and they scan the room, resting on everyone for a moment.

I guess the thing I notice and respect most about her is that she does not stoop under the weight of their stares; she stands tall and proud. When they stare, she stares right back.

A whisper of "nigger" goes around the room, not loud enough for the teacher to hear, but there all the same. I say nothing, although tears are burning behind my eyes and I seethe with unseen anger. They are not even giving her a chance!

Then I smile, the least bit. Now there is someone else like me. Maybe together we can stand them.

ABOUT THE AUTHOR

Koren Ziemienski lives in West Allis, Wisconsin. She is a student at the Horace Mann Middle School, also in West Allis.

Old traditions, new friends, and a summer ritual.

Beginnings and Ends

by *ADAM SCHWARTZ*

In the distance, an old man chants in a preternatural voice, "Whata Hata Ho-ooo." We all respond to the mysterious voice by echoing the same words. Jingling bells signal the approach of a young lad costumed in war paint and an Indian headdress. The youthful brave nods to us, and we understand that we are to follow him through the woods, embarking on an unknown adventure. The Indian, too, wonders what the setting sun will bring as he diligently walks barefoot over rocky paths and prickly pine needles. We approach the area together, although a few stragglers lag behind. Do they stop to pick up something they have dropped, or have they slowed their pace to think for a moment about this very special night? When we arrive at our destination, we spy other groups of children who are already sitting on black wooden benches, quietly awaiting the program. Our group stakes out a place and sits down, some on the cold ground and others on the splintered benches. Meanwhile, our Indian guide proceeds to the front to stand with the other Indian leaders.

The landscape is magnificent. The lake flows gently behind the Indians, its waves rolling into shore. An occasional raucous motorboat causes a disturbance on the peaceful water. The grand coniferous trees, each with its own history and memories, stand behind the benches like soldiers, lining the sky. Paper bags weighted with sand and a single candle dot the shoreline. There is a small log cabin constructed of wood in an old ash-filled fire pit, but the fire has not yet been started. The sky turns from deep blue to pale black as the fiery orange sun begins to set over the lake.

Suddenly, all is quiet as an Indian with a majestic headdress beats a large animal skin tom-tom. A soothing voice tells an ancient Indian legend as a few Indians pantomime the tale: There once was an old Indian who was always melancholy. He was the God of Winter, and he lived in a fortress surrounded by huge ice walls. He had plagued the area with ice and snow for many years, destroying all the crops. A young brave was sent to stop this old man. He was the God of Summer, but he had little power at the time. He traveled to the man's fortress and timidly knocked on the door. As he walked in, his heat began to melt the walls. The God of Winter was enraged, but he could not stop the young brave. The old man melted too, and the God of Summer once again became powerful.

The story ends, but no applause is heard. Though everyone has enjoyed the dramatic narrative, this event is too serious for applause or laughter. Only silence comes from the captive audience.

A young counselor walks in front of the unlit fire. Magically, he produces a spark from his hands. He casts the flame so that it gently descends into the calm lake and then is extinguished. The campers are astounded. This tall and strong-willed counselor begins to speak. Slowly, but loudly, he recites a poem which introduces the theme of the night: "Beginnings and Ends." The poem seems to flow like the lake, these first few words of a long, wonderful night yet to come. We are overwhelmed by the way the words seem to wrap us up and carry us away to a land that only we can see. All is quiet again as the counselor concludes his poem and reclines on the sacred ground. Very young campers use him as a pillow, for it is already eight o'clock and they are tired.

As we peer out over the lake, a canoe bearing a lighted torch drifts near. The dark red sun has almost set, and all is calm. The vessel glides closer to the fire area, until the older campers in the canoe can wade to shore and into the Council Ring. They bring with them the flaming torch to light the fire. The torch touches the logs and the wood bursts into flames. As the torch is extinguished in the lake, the first few brave sparks shoot out of the fire and float into the night-time sky. Now the true council fire can begin.

A camper with a guitar walks to the fire and kneels down. He lays some music on the ground, knowing the fire will illuminate the notes. As he plays, everyone listens: "Now my son was born just the other day/He learned to walk while I was away . . ." As some mysterious musical force comes over the campers, they join in harmony for the chorus: "And the cat's in the cradle and the silver spoon/Little Boy Blue and the man in the moon . . ." The song fades into silence as two other campers step forward. This is their first council fire, so they are timid and shy. They speak quietly as they read a poem that they wrote during rest period. The poem relates to their first few days at camp.

As darkness descends upon the land, more campers and counselors recite speeches, read poems, and sing songs. By now the sun has set, and the fire dances up into the sky. Some campers stare at the candles, which create mysterious bouncing patterns in the paper bags. Others count the waves as they gently touch the shore. A slight breeze begins to stir the leaves, and spooky noises can be heard.

Thoughts are abruptly interrupted by the slow, even bass notes of the Indian drum. The archery specialist steps before the fire, crossbow in hand. As an ancient poem about an honest warrior who never misses his mark is recited, he draws an arrow from the bag slung over his shoulder and holds the tip in the fire. When he pulls it out, the tip sizzles and glows. He draws back the bow and, when the poem is finished, lets the arrow fly across the lake. The sparks create a trail which streaks through the night. Two more arrows are released, and they too make trails of fire.

As the evening draws to a close and the fire slowly dies, a counselor known for his singing steps in front of the fire. The sky is pitch-black by now, and all that is visible are the moonlit tops of trees. This counselor plays his guitar and begins to sing a traditional camp song: "The whispering of trees, the haunting melodies . . ." Everyone is familiar with this song, for it has been sung time and again by campers and counselors, young and old. I am seated next to a child whose father composed this beautiful haunting melody twenty-three summers ago. We all join in to sing the chorus one last time, softly, slowly, as one unified group bonded by a feeling of mutual friendship: "Thunderbird, what you are, stretches near and far/You stretch your fingers and you'll send/Strong young boys to proud young men."

The song's profoundly moving words fade away as one last poem is read by the program director. Finally, the council fire ends with the traditional practice of making a friendship circle, a chain of crossing arms right over left and holding hands with the people on either side. "Taps" is played, and we all sing "Living in Tents and Cabins." Then the camp director shares a traditional Irish prayer: "May the road always rise up to meet you . . ." We chorus, "Sing your way home at the end of the day. Smile all the way, send your troubles away . . ." The songs we have sung, the poems I have heard, the thoughts that other campers have expressed affect me deeply.

Candles lead the way up spooky, rocky paths as we return to our cabins.

ABOUT THE AUTHOR

Adam Schwartz attends Sycamore Jr. High School in Cincinnati, Ohio. His hobbies range from playing the piano to Rollerblading. He is active in student government and writes for his school newspaper, The Flyer.

Close to Home

Memories of a brother—and a friend.

Blank Disks

by MORGAN HEINTZ

I remember back to two years ago . . . He sat there in the wooden chair, bonded to the Macintosh by the white glare of the screen reflected onto his face. His fingers typed furiously, then slowed down. He thought, biting his upper lip, closing his eyes, his head tilted back. And then . . . Wham! His eyelids sprinted back, revealing life, exhilaration. He typed again, now more wildly, rushing, making sure that he got all his ideas on the screen before he forgot them.

I remember back to two years ago . . . The sound of the ImageWriter creeping through my door— *connnndggo-in-do-ee!*—as I tried to sleep. I see the carriage sliding across the paper, leaving tracks of words from my brother's English report, then sliding back to the left and beginning again.

I remember back to two years ago . . . Walking into the small room with the windows on three of the four sides. The sun leaked through mini-blinds, bringing life and energy into the room. I brought my brother Nestlé chocolate chip cookies, warm from the first batch that I had just baked from scratch—a studying high school student's vital survival food.

But that was when he was a part of Ms. Busy's English class.

My brother is leaving now. Accepted at Trinity College.

"Everything is packed," he says. When he says everything, he means tapes, posters, compact disks, stereo system, and some cologne to attract the girls.

We sent him his forgotten toothbrush.

Dad drove, Mom tried to tell old stories: "Remember the time you cut your hair and said that you were going to fire your old barber? . . ." Grover tried to sleep but I poked him, tickled him—anything to stop him from going to sleep and leaving me and his old life at home before we had to say goodbye. And even after that, I chased him to the dorm.

We went home. I cried while my parents thought I was sleeping under my jacket.

My brother is gone now. Off to college. He's taken the computer to his dorm room. I don't hear him typing anymore. He has graduated from his senior European History class—no more midnight essays to write.

My brother is gone now. Off to college. He has taken the ImageWriter, too. Falling asleep should be easy now. I have nothing to distract me but fond memories. And wishes.

My brother is gone now. Off to college. He's taken himself. Away. As I walk into the computer room, it's no longer a place I go to laugh. No glow fills the air, no cookie crumbs on the floor for Mom to yell about, no Grover. I have tried to fix it up. I have painted it, got a new floor, hung a picture of a beach scene, bought an upholstered chair, and even put in a bookshelf with colorful books that I don't read. Nothing can make it as special as it used to be.

My brother is gone now. Off to college. Cookies aren't very fun to bake when you have only yourself to share them with. Grover's not there anymore. No friendly person with eyes full of thanks, no brother smiling and telling me he'll do anything that I want for the rest of my life and that I'll always be his life-saver.

ABOUT THE AUTHOR

Morgan Heintz attends Weston Middle School in Weston, Massachusetts. She writes: "I'm always up for a vicious game of field hockey or soccer. I love to go for a sunfish sail or windsurf until I collapse into my bed. And if I'm not doing any of that, or saving dolphins, or studying, I'm probably tickling my brother!"

From a bird that wouldn't die, a lesson in courage.

The Cormorant in My Bathtub

by BROOKE ROGERS

When I was about eight, I went to live with my grandparents at the beach. I had never seen the ocean before, and to this day the memory is vivid. We pulled into the driveway at dusk, and I could see behind the house an exciting expanse of untouched water. I shivered. Since my parents died, I had not felt any emotion; I had been only a breathing vegetable. But now I could feel the blood beginning to pump through my veins. I felt warm and tingly. The colors of the horizon and the dying sun were a shimmer of pinks and purples. The sun, arrayed in its most beautiful gown, was ready to die valiantly. I was sure even the Garden of Eden could not have been more beautiful.

From that moment on I was madly in love with the ocean. I lay in the sand for hours watching the cormorants circling over the lapping waves. How I envied those birds, their graceful black bodies circling and diving into the brilliant waters. They did not know fear or sadness; they knew only life, sun, and the ocean. They would plummet into the sea at tremendous speeds, and not once did they miss their prey. There were no failures. Each one always emerged with a silver minnow speared on its beak.

Every day from sunup to sundown I haunted the beach. I never tried to make new friends; I was always alone. I dreaded the first day of school. I was always dreaming that I would become a cormorant and fly away over the ocean, never to be seen again.

It was a Wednesday night when the tanker sank. The rain was falling in solid sheets, the wind blowing at nearly fifty knots! All the power lines were out; even the glow of the lighthouse was not strong enough to pierce the storm. The captain of the tanker lost his course and ran aground on Lookout Point. The side of the tanker split on the rocks, spilling hundreds of thousands of gallons of oil into the raging sea.

The next day the ocean was calm, but the waves that lapped against the beach were tainted. Riding on the waves were the black remains of the oil tanker's cargo. I watched in horror as helpless sea birds struggled to stay afloat, flapping their wings in frenzied splashes as they tried desperately to free themselves from the clinging oil. Tears streamed down my cheeks as I dashed into the ocean and gathered up as many birds as I could capture. I returned to the house and filled the bathtub with clean, fresh water. Then I pried open as many beaks as I could. I watched helplessly as the birds surrendered to the clinging grease that clogged their nostrils and held fast their beaks. My whole body shook with grief. I lifted their limp bodies and tenderly set them on a towel. Among the dead were three gulls, two sandpipers, and one brown pelican.

One bird remained in the tub, a black bird who would not give up. He lay quietly in the tub, but his eyes were alert, and he was wide awake. He was a cormorant. To take my mind off the others, I picked him up and began to rub his back with tissue and detergent. It took hours, but the bird seemed to sense that I was trying to help. He lay still and allowed me to wipe every last drop of oil off his glossy back. When I placed him back in the tub he drank deeply, enjoying the strange, sweet taste of fresh water for the first time.

When my grandma found me she did not scold me for making a mess of her guest bathroom. She simply asked if I would like some help burying the dead birds. Without asking, I knew she would let the cormorant stay in her bathtub. The bird was clearly exhausted. He lay motionless with his head tucked under his wing. As we buried the six birds, I wondered what would happen to the seventh.

For a week my grandparents forbade me to visit the beach. I knew that the oil was still thick and that the white sand would never be quite as pure. We had numerous wildlife representatives visit our beach and collect water samples and gather up dead fish and birds. They would often stop and look in on my bird, but they never tried to take him away. I fed him sardines and tuna fish. He ate greedily and slowly became stronger. Sadly, I realized that my new friend would need to leave me.

A few kids in my neighborhood stopped by to see

the bird. Grandma encouraged them to stay for tea, and I was surprised at how much fun we had. The more time I spent with the neighborhood kids, the more I looked forward to the opening of school. The water was regaining its purity and soon it would be safe to let my bird go. He would once again be searching the sea for a school of minnows instead of splashing about in our bathtub. Still, I did not like to think about losing him.

Two weeks after the storm, school started. I was excited by new classes and new friends. I was spending very little time on the beach. Instead, I had been playing baseball in the lot behind our house. I felt needed and wanted for the first time since my parents' death; the black bird in my bathtub needed me, and my friends wanted me to play third base and share adventures with them.

On the third day of school I returned home to find the bird gone. The door was shut tight, but the window was open and the curtain was blowing in the breeze. On the floor below the window a long black feather rested. I picked it up and stroked the smooth edge as I thought of all the bird had given me.

ABOUT THE AUTHOR

Brooke Rogers lives in Olympia, Washington, and attends Charles Wright Academy in Tacoma. She has a collection of pets, including two dogs, two ducks, one hamster, one rabbit, and three cats.

Sometimes life happens by accident . . .

Passing Time

by CHAD MORRIS

The month of June: a time that a friend tried to imitate Ludwig van Beethoven, my Irish setter ate most of our wheat and barley, and my mom studied Archimedes' mathematical concepts. She also read a great number of poetic novels by John Steinbeck and studied ancient fossils that could possibly exist beneath our farm. Dad was sort of loony and tried killing and skinning diamondback rattlesnakes. My brother, whom I considered mentally retarded, stayed inside his room practicing yoga. And me, well, I would usually just lie in the fields of gold and waste time, listening to the mockingbirds mock the crows. Sometimes, though, it would seem that they were laughing at *me*.

The sun shined upon the hide of our cow's back, making its way up above the bristle-pointed treetops. The wind made the leather that held my moccasins together flap, and the Bermuda grass of refreshing green swayed. The quail that lived by my pond shattered my eardrums with the awful noise they made, sending electric streams of icicle chips running down my spine.

"Mom, I'm going to meet Beethoven, I mean Benny, at the pond. I'll be home sometime tonight," I said.

"OK, but be careful. Remember—after the first death, there is no other."

I took my daily stroll down the path of darkness and knew that at the other end would be two friends waiting, Benny and the pond. As I looked ahead, watching for potholes, I saw the zinnias swaying in the wind and heard the umbrella bird crying its awful cry, and the wind cooled my head from the immense heat.

At last I arrived, discovering an unimaginable sight. My head started spinning and my mouth started watering as Benny introduced me to Renea. My knees suddenly felt like rubber and my hands got clammy. The wind kept on trying to cool my head from the immense heat.

After I finally pulled myself together, I noticed that this girl wasn't just one of your typical everyday semi-pretty passersby that you see in school all the time. After debating over what we were going to do for the next thirty minutes, we decided to climb the oak tree at the beginning of the path leading to Benny's house.

We started walking, but of course Benny had to be the first one up, so he dashed toward it. Renea trailed behind, keeping her distance, but making sure she didn't fall too far behind. By the time I arrived at the tree, Benny was already halfway up, acting like a gorilla, swinging from branch to branch. Renea followed behind him, again keeping her distance. As I started climbing the tree, a branch that Renea was standing on gave way, and she fell with it, crying a scream of death like Satan calling a demon. Acting upon instinct, I stepped back onto the ground and broke her fall, but her head still hit hard on the black concrete, knocking her unconscious.

This was the moment I had waited for all my life! Here I was, holding the most beautiful girl I had ever seen in my entire life (not including my mother). One slight problem, though, made me wish this hadn't happened. What should I do? Should I put her down and let her regain consciousness, or keep holding her till she woke up? This was a Kodak moment that I'd never forget, especially because of not knowing what to do. My mind fluttered off in a million directions, some thoughts wise, some ordinary, and some ridiculous.

Benny, somewhat in shock, quickly pulled her from my arms and dragged her to the edge of the pond, where he sprinkled her face with water. He continued scooping out the water and letting it splash in her face. After he dumped about a million gallons of muddy pond slime onto her face, she came to. Benny was just about as relieved as Renea to find that we had actually helped her.

I wish now, in retrospect, that Benny had never brought Renea to the pond. I had planned on swimming or something like that, WITHOUT someone else tagging along. Well, my perfectly planned-out day wasn't going to be ruined by one careless little girl . . .

We decided to paddle across the pond in our homemade canoe. As we started nearing the middle—the deepest area—I asked to head back, but they just made fun of me and started rocking the canoe. And in one split second, it tipped over. *Crraackkk!*

This all happened, oh, about three days ago, and now I'm here in my room with nothing to do. I am forbidden to go back to the pond, and it'll be a few days before I am allowed to see Benny again.

My mom explained that I had fallen out of the canoe and hit my head on a rock. Evidently, the rock overcame my ability to retain consciousness, and I passed out when my oxygen supply was cut off by the water. Luckily, Benny knows some lifesaving maneuvers and managed to pull me out. Then he ran and got my dad.

So now I'm in bed with only memories to play with. The sun still shines upon my fields of gold; the wind still lifts the immense heat from the earth, cooling it to a mere 100 degrees; Dad stills tends the farm and drives the livestock almost as crazy as he is; Mom still makes, in Dad's words, "the most luscious, mouth-watering pie in this here county"; the dog still chews on our half-eaten crops; Benny still waits by the pond, thinking that I'll be healed in a day, like a miracle sent from God or something; and I, the only living person in the entire universe who can't still perform his daily routine, lie here in bed with only memories to play with. Ah, well—such is life. Relaxing now, my eyes slowly close, and my mind drifts off to Never-Never Land.

ABOUT THE AUTHOR

Chad Morris lives in Baytown, Texas, and attends George H. Gentry Junior School, also in Baytown. Interested in electronic technology, he spends his free time "fooling around" on his computer, playing computer games, and learning more about computers.

Has she discovered a new species of domestic pest?

Televisionus Maximus

by LAURA FOX

Plopped on the couch beside me is the *Televisionus Maximus*, transfixed by the television set. I probe it closely with my eyes. Yes, there cannot exist a more fascinating animal for the purpose of my study. *Maximus* is the sole animal that can actually be defined as "addicted to television." The inner brain consists of a complicated and inhuman jumble of wires and flashing images. The constant need for TV is programmed into this creature by the television itself in flashing picture codes. It actually communicates personally with the TVs in the household. These conversations cannot yet be translated, but there are linguists presently working on it.

Mutation into the *Maximus* state can be prevented by isolating the prospective *Maximus* from communication with any working television for eight weeks, preferably by sending it to summer camp. If you think you live with a future *Maximus*, watch for its unmistakable method of feeding on, or "watching," TV. It will sit for as long as possible, eyes set, feet apart, undisturbable, singing along with the commercials hypnotically. Look into its eyes deeply and you will actually see the pink, blue, red, and yellow images being absorbed. Its voice will match that of the person singing the commercial ditty, and you will hear it singing these ditties in order at the dinner table, or in other places. It is entranced.

If extended periods of this kind of viewing are not available, it may show symptoms of TVlackasitis. This disease is not uncommon among *Maximi* and is occasioned by chronic lack of TV. At the onset of this disease, *T. Maximus* rushes the TV set and thrusts its dirty, chubby appendages at the power button, only to be forcibly stopped. Then it sounds its warning call, "IwannawatchTVIwannawatchTV!" This alarms anyone in the area, including the Household King or Queen. Next it unleashes a big, wailing fit, writhing spasmodically on the floor until it is certain that every member of the household is watching. It directs its greatest spasms toward a sympathetic adult. This impresses everyone so much that it is allowed to feed until it is no longer hungry. Approximate feeding time is ten hours. During these precious hours of feeding, it will watch anything. It may even watch the news or the Spanish channel, the *Maximi* equivalent of Brussels sprouts or cauliflower.

There is usually one in every home. They are six to nine years old and have no homework, chores, or other responsibilities, and their schedules are built around the TV. They are closely related to the *Nintendus Maximus*. Both species are commonly known as "little brothers."

ABOUT THE AUTHOR

Laura Fox is a student at Weston Middle School in Weston, Massachusetts. Along with writing, her hobbies include swimming, performing in musical plays, and going on hiking and camping trips—"with my friends, not my family," she clarifies.

Her love reached across miles—and generations.

Po

by ABRAHAM TZOU

I was only two and one-half months old when I first met Po. The time was November, 1978; the place was Grandpa's house in Taipei, Taiwan. My mom took me with her to Taiwan for a visit; she could not wait to show off her brand-new baby boy to all the friends and relatives back home. At first sight, Po picked me up from Mom's arms as if I were Po's first-born. I made quite an impression on everybody there because I was crying as if I had been stabbed by a sharp pin. Having just been on a fifteen-hour overseas flight, Mom was too exhausted to calm me down. So Po volunteered to hold me and to cuddle me so that Mom could get some rest. Walking and rocking me back and forth in the living room throughout the night, Po was finally able to put me to sleep. Po must have had very sore arms and feet that first time we met! Although I was too young to actually remember anything from this particular episode, I could just picture it in my mind years later when Mom told me about it.

My next close encounter with Po took place when I was two years old. Mom was offered a teaching position at a private university in Taiwan. Since Dad had to finish up his Ph.D. at the University of Illinois, he suggested that Mom accept the offer and take me back to Taiwan with her. We stayed at Grandpa's four-bedroom condominium in Taipei. Po lived there, too.

I had a severe nose-bleeding problem at that time. For some unknown reason, my nose would bleed heavily at least two or three times a day. Both Mom and Po were very worried. Mom took me to many doctors, but none of them seemed to help. Po asked around among friends and found out about an experienced Chinese herbal doctor. Mom decided to give it a try. After the herbal doctor had felt my pulse from both wrists, he started prescribing on a piece of $8^1/2''$ by $11''$ letter-size paper, using a brush pen to write all kinds of small Chinese characters. Mom told me that there were at least twenty-some herbs included in the prescription. But that was nothing compared to what we had to do with the prescription afterwards!

Mom brought home a huge bag of herbs which had been cautiously scaled and mixed and individually packed and sealed at the herb store. To get up at four o'clock in the morning and start simmering one pack of the herbs for four hours every day became a ritual for Mom and Po. It was extremely important that the heat and the amount of water be just right at all times so that the final product would be most effective. Since Mom had a busy schedule at the university, Po volunteered to do it all alone so that Mom could concentrate on her teaching commitment.

It was, however, an absolute nightmare for me to have to drink, three times a day after meals, the dark brown liquid extracted from all the herbs. I'm sure it was the most horrible-tasting medicine that anybody has ever had to take. The mission was almost impossible, especially since I was only two years old and was way beyond reasoning. It took Po unbelievable effort and patience to get the precious medicine carefully prepared; it took Po still more in the way of creativity, along with some magic, to actually manage to get the yucky liquid successfully transferred from the elegant rice bowl into that stubborn little mouth of mine, three times a day! By the end of the eighth month, I was completely cured. Po, on the other hand, had lost about twenty pounds and gained an alarmingly high blood pressure in return.

My path and Po's have crossed many more times since then. After fulfilling her one-year teaching obligation, Mom was given charge of occasional short-term projects at the university. She took me back to Taiwan at least once a year on assignment, and we got to spend a lot of time with Po on each visit. Every time we came back to the States, our suitcases would be overflowing with food, clothes, and toys that Po had bought for us. When Po saw us off at the airport, I could not hide my feelings very well. Trying to cheer me up, Po said, "Don't be sad, Abe. We'll see each other again, sooner than you think. Besides, we'll always be together in our hearts . . ." However, I detected some shakiness in Po's voice and tears in Po's eyes.

Po was invited by Mom and Dad to come visit us in the States. I was so excited that I could not sleep the night before. The day Po arrived, Mom and Dad took me to pick up Po at the San Francisco International Airport. I was going to give Po a big hug, but Po called out, "Oh, be careful, Abe. I've got my hands full!" In Po's hands was my favorite Chinese pastry that weighed about thirty pounds. Po had insisted on hand-carrying it halfway around the world so that the delicious and delicate pastry would stay fresh and look nice, not squeezed or smashed.

I could just write a whole book about the nice things that Po has done for me, but I can never fully express my appreciation for Po. Po is the most caring and loving person that I have ever known, besides my own parents.

By the way, Po is seventy-two years old now. She is the mother of my mother. As a matter of fact, "Po" is the phonetic translation of the Chinese word for "Grandma."

ABOUT THE AUTHOR

Born in Illinois, Abraham Tzou is a bilingual Chinese-American. He attends Ralston Middle School in Belmont, California. Abraham enjoys playing the piano and drawing; favorite sports are baseball, basketball, and football.

Being sick was hard. Being lonely was worse . . .

The Campfire

by AIMEE SOWARDS

rian Dyer is dying, thought Brian as he plopped down on the dirty camp bunk. No one else was in the small room. He was all alone, as he thought he had been all his life.

Brian wasn't sure how he had gotten lung cancer. He was only fifteen and he had never smoked, though both his mother and his father did. But he didn't want to think about his parents right now. They were the ones who sent him off to this horrible camp. They thought he needed a break from it all. He didn't belong here. This was a place for normal people. People who weren't dying.

The only thing that kept him going was the eighteen-year-old counselor named Tiffany. She was very pretty, and he always saw her around the pool and campfire.

A knock on the door broke his thoughts. "Come in," Brian said dully.

"Hi." It was Tiffany. Brian's face brightened immediately, but Tiffany didn't notice.

"Hi, Tif! What's up?" Brian said with a smile.

"I was wondering if you would like to sing and toast marshmallows by the campfire. Everyone is there but you."

"I'll be there in a minute."

"OK." She quietly turned and left.

He walked out the door behind her. When he got to the campfire, he stood just outside the circle of laughing people. He looked around for Tiffany and saw that she had her arms around two guys. It was perfectly innocent. But Brian took it the wrong way; he thought she was doing it just to hurt him.

Brian quickly walked away. He headed for the lake. As he sat on the dock, he started to think that he wasn't successful at anything. Girls, friends, or even life. He stood up on the dock and jumped.

The last sounds he heard were the laughter around the campfire, a splash, and then silence. Total silence.

ABOUT THE AUTHOR

Aimee Sowards is a student at Prospect Heights Middle School in Orange, Virginia. She reports: "I love to read, play with Buffy (my dog), and watch TV."

Would loving someone new
mean forgetting his mom?

The End of the Beginning

by SIANA COLLYER

D ad was depressed for a year after Mom died. Even for me, Matt, his only son, it's embarrassing to admit some of the things that his depression made him do.

First of all, before Mom died, he always used to play with the twins, Sarah and Liz, my younger sisters. He would piggyback them all around the place and patiently let them dress him up when they played house and all that. Then Mom got an inoperable brain tumor. Inoperable because the doctors found it too late. She died last fall. Dad suddenly neglected the twins as if they were icicles and he, a shivering Hawaiian. Sarah started bringing home bad grades, and Liz began to get into more and more trouble at school. But did Dad notice? No. I had to handle it. You can imagine how tough it was for a fourteen-year-old to try to talk some sense into a group of condescending first-grade teachers.

And Maxine. She is—or was—our French housekeeper. Whenever she cooked a meal, Dad would put down his fork and sigh dramatically, "It's good, I suppose, but Lise made it much better."

Maxine handed in her resignation. She said she was fed up with us. Or something like that. She said it in French, which I had a little trouble understanding: I hate to admit that I got a C- on my French midterm.

So while Dad moped at work, came home and moped, and moped in his sleep, I had to juggle cleaning, cooking, laundry, the twins' affairs, then try to squeeze in homework and swimming at Cotch Pool.

It was Thursday night, and I'd made sure that all the chores were finished good and early. That way, I could make popcorn for the twins, and we'd all watch "The Cosby Show" before I'd put them to bed.

Dad came bursting through the door, singing "Next Time I Fall in Love" by Peter Cetera. It was off-key, and I was about to offer my Peter Cetera tape. Sarah was staring at Dad, and Liz flung herself into his arms. Dad hugged us all in turn and then said, "What's Maxy-baby fixed for sup tonight?"

I grinned and the twins groaned.

"Maxine quit last week, Dad," I said.

Dad looked at me for a minute, then laughed and got his coat back on.

"I guess it's dinner with the Swansons tonight, kids. Come on, Matt, let's go get some TV dinners."

I knew there was a new woman in Dad's life. Lately, I had been reading books by Dr. Jonas Birdwhistle. (Don't laugh—that's really his name!) Dr. J. said that men whose spouses or partners have died or have left them are living without adequate female companionship. They need a woman in their lives to keep them healthy.

I realized that the reason Grandpa Barney's health had gone downhill last year was because of Grandma Lizzie's death.

On the way to Super Stop & Shop, I was quiet in the car. Dad asked me if I was OK.

"Yeah, Dad. I—I'm just glad you're back on track again. Uh, I haven't gone to the pool lately. Could we go tonight? It's a three-day weekend, and all of my homework is done."

Dad began to look very vague, kind of staring into space. Suddenly the car swerved. A man in a blue Chevette yelled, "Watch where yer goin', buddy!"

Dad gripped the wheel and looked at me.

"Sure, Matt. I know your laps are important. Do you mind if I bring along a new friend of mine?"

This was where I had to start watching myself. If Dad was going to replace Mom, I'd have to approve. So would the twins.

"Uh, yeah sure, Dad. Who is it?"

"Rebecca Sprague-Allen. She's very sweet . . ." his voice trailed off.

"Do you call her"—*gulp*—"Becky?"

"Yes. That's what I call her."

Dad parked the car and we headed for the shopping carts. He had a faraway look in his eyes as we wandered through the aisles. I didn't ask any more questions about this new woman, but that look in his eyes made me eager to see what our evening at the pool would bring.

She was beautiful—tall, like Dad, and like Mom. But my mixed feelings toward Becky were quickly apparent. I was still feeling faithful to Mom and missing her. I loved my mom a lot. Of course, I never admitted that to the guys on my basketball team, or to Billy Kane, my best pal who had moved to Houston: that would be very uncool. But I knew that all the other guys loved their moms, and there had been a lot of sympathizing around school when my mom died.

Becky wore a plain, one-piece black suit that showed all her curves. Mom had had curves. Well, some. She liked to bake after a hard day at the office (she was a lawyer), and more often than not, she was her own guinea pig for those baking experiments.

Becky smelled nice, too. Like a basket of flowers. Mom had smelled like lavender and Irish clover. Chalk up another point—Becky was at a tie with Mom.

Becky dressed fashionably. So did Mom.

Becky was gentle and kind, not really flirtatious. I'd thought that since she could inspire Dad to sing "Next Time I Fall," she might be a flirt. But she wasn't, and she seemed to make Dad very happy.

The twins liked her, too. Sarah and Liz got dolphin rides around the pool. Becky divided her time between us and Dad. No, actually, she divided her time between the twins and Dad. I tried to look as busy as possible practicing laps. I stayed above water only long enough to breathe, defog my goggles, and make sure that Becky was keeping her distance. She was always at the other end of the pool, and I decided that if Becky was going to stay, she was going to have to acknowledge my existence.

My best friend, next to Billy Kane, had always been Amanda Webster. I mean, so what if she was a girl? I could talk unreservedly with her. Amanda was also a fashion expert. Dad usually gave me money to do the twins' clothes shopping, so whenever it came to that time, I would call Amanda, collect the twins, and we'd all hop a bus to our sister city, Penelope, where the mall was.

Last year, we'd had a frightening experience. Amanda and Liz and I were walking through the mall with Sarah wandering along behind us. Some thug jumped out and tried to take Amanda's handbag. Amanda pulled it back and started beating the kid over the head with it. He was shielding himself with a hand and shouting, "Get away from me! Get *away* from me!"

He was from the rough side of town, and a gang emblem—a cobra—was stitched on his jean jacket.

Amanda grabbed a ceramic vase from a display cart and smashed it over his head. He was knocked out. All the while Sarah and Liz were clinging to me. Sarah stepped forward and looked, like a lovelorn puppy, into Amanda's face.

"You better marry Matt when you grow up 'cause Matt would be too scared to do that!"

They say that fools and children speak the truth.

There were several articles in the paper after that, and Amanda got a Medal of Merit from Mayor Flannery. That was the end of it. Amanda's not that big on publicity.

It had been a month since Dad started seeing Becky, and he had decided that the twins needed new clothes. Becky was over for breakfast that day, and she hadn't said much to me, except for a few futile attempts at conversation. These were killed by a cold, unreceptive glance from me. *Oh, Becky*, I thought, grappling for control of my heart, *can't you see why I can't get close?*

When I went out to the hall to phone Amanda's house, I heard Becky say to my father, "Peter, don't you think the girls should have a woman shop for them? I could do it."

I gritted my teeth so hard (I later found out, painfully, at the dentist's office) that a tooth had to be fixed.

Silence. Dad said, "No, Becky. Even when Lise was alive, she let Amanda and Matt take the girls out. Kind of a home economics they were never taught in school."

I breathed a sigh of relief. Thanks, Dad.

"Webster residence." Oh no—Amanda's little brother, Timothy.

"Yeah, this is Matt. Can I talk to Amanda?" I coughed and shuffled my feet. I hate Timothy. He's a brat.

Timothy dropped the phone with a clunk and screamed, " 'Manda! It's your *boyfriend, Matt!*" I swear, the kid must intentionally put his mouth right on the receiver to yell "boyfriend Matt" so loud.

"Shut up, Tim, and will you kindly remove your teeth from the phone cord?" I heard Amanda growl.

"Hi, Matt. What's up?" She sounded just like always, affable and pleasant and comfortable. (Not like this weirdo that Josh Duncan once tried to fix me up with. Alice Peasley. She mumbled on the phone, "I—I—I just want to be cool." She was a loser. Girls that mumble and stutter on the phone turn me off.)

"The twins need some clothes. Do you want to go to the mall at around three?"

"How could I refuse, Matt? I need a sweater anyway, and I have to pick up a few things from the drugstore."

"Which bus stop do you want to take? Countryside or Vineyard?"

"Vineyard is closer to your place, Matt. Anyway, I need the exercise. I'm starting to be able to pinch a centimeter or two."

I started to protest. Girls have a thing about getting fat, I guess. Just like guys worry about zits. There's this one kid in my class, Eddie. A real basket-case juvenile delinquent. He'll go up to a teacher with an apple, pledge his eternal devotion, and ask to cut class. Or, he'll go up to a couple at a dance and push the guy across the floor. (Eddie is about 5'11" and around 1,000 tons.) He dances with the cowering girl until he gets tired and pushes *her* across the room, too. His face looks like the sky on a starry night—covered with hordes of little flaming zits.

"Matt?" Amanda said.

"What?"

"Shut up," she replied good-naturedly.

I grinned and put down the receiver.

A couple of hours later, we were in Jordan Marsh. Amanda was regarding a three-way reflection of herself in a pair of Guess jeans.

"I don't know, Matt. They kind of overlap around the ankles." She blinked. "What do you think?"

I had been staring at Amanda for a while, noticing how graceful and beautiful she was, and how I had never appreciated it before.

I blinked.

"Yeah—they uh—look a little strange." If Amanda had noticed my cover-up, she didn't show it.

"You're right," she said. "I'm sorry to drag you

around like this when I really only needed a sweater."
She looked at me carefully and paused. "Matt, is every-
thing OK at home? I mean, with Becky and your dad?
I get the feeling you don't like her that much."

I looked at Amanda and decided to confide in her.

"I don't want to get close to her, Amanda. I know
this is stupid, but I feel like . . . like I'll lose my mom—
wherever she is—if I like Becky too much. I just . . . I
mean, do you know what I mean?" There wasn't even
a hint of a giggle around Amanda's face.

"I think I do." Before we left the three-way mir-
ror, Amanda turned my shoulders toward her and said
in an unusually soft voice, "Hey, Matt, I want you to
know that I'm always here for you."

"Thanks a lot, Amanda. I feel better. It's nice to
know that I've got a friend like you."

We were finished with all of our shopping, so I
bought Sarah and Liz each an ice cream cone from
Camille's On Wheels, an ice cream vendor boasting
fifty-eight flavors. The twins sat by a bubbling foun-
tain that has this statue of the Independent Man. He's
a tarnished-gold color, and he has a piece of cloth
around his waist that kind of looks like the wind blew
it there. He has a pitchfork or something in his hand,
and he looks cold every time you see him, if you ask
me.

I walked Amanda to the front door of her house.
While she fumbled for a key (because her parents and
brother had gone out), she said, "Matt, thank you for
such a nice time. You and the twins are so much fun
to be around—especially compared to My Brother from
Mars. Call me again sometime."

"I will. Thanks, Amanda. I mean, it's really great

of you to help me with the clothes bit. I kind of didn't want Becky to break our tradition. *She* wanted to take the twins out—instead of you and me."

Amanda looked up. A lock of her short, soft, wavy hair fell over her eye. She brushed it away, and I got the full span of her time-lapse smile.

"See you later, Amanda."

"Bye, Matt. Thank you."

I headed down the street, reluctantly. But I quickened my pace when I found it was 5:00 P.M. Becky was coming over within the half-hour, and I wanted to make it up to my room before she arrived.

Rap-rap-rap.

"Matt? It's Dad. Can I come in? I'd like to talk to you."

I turned away from my telescope. I'd been following a trawler moving out to sea from the bay. "Yeah, I guess." Dad came in and eased himself down on my bed. I knew what was coming.

"Matt, what's going on with Becky? I've gone over this many, many times in my head, trying to see what you see wrong with her. I come up with zilch. Think you can help me?"

All of a sudden, the bag inside me which held all that hurt and grief and the feeling of Becky intruding on me and my still grieving over Mom tore open and blasted a tempest into my throat.

"Dammit, Dad!" I yelled furiously. "Becky never even comes *near* me!"

"You dug your own grave with that, Matt. You've brushed her off."

I went on recklessly. "Becky loves the twins! Becky even wanted to break my tradition with Amanda. God,

Dad, if you had wanted to pick a *replacement* for Mom, couldn't you have picked a good one?" Tears flooded my eyes. "I *can't* like Becky! I'd . . . I'd be . . . betraying Mom."

The lines that had furrowed Dad's forehead disappeared.

"Matt, has this been what's wrong? You think you're betraying Mom? I'm going to tell you something that I have never told anyone—not even Becky.

"In those last few minutes I had with Mom, she said to me, 'Peter, when I am gone, I will wait for you. But find a woman to make you and our children happy. It's all I want.'" Dad's eyes watered while he said it. Then, very quietly, he whispered, "I could never replace Mom. She was one of a kind, and I loved her very, very much. I know you did, too. Becky is helping me overcome my grief over losing Mom, and she's helping me to live again. Becky was scared off by you— so much so that she wouldn't make a move."

I felt drained. Becky *wasn't* a replacement. She was an addition. This changed things a whole lot. I felt foolish. Dad hugged me.

"Matt, accepting change is something we all go through. Birth, death, and everything in between involves change. Adding Becky to our lives is a change. How do you feel?"

"Better."

"Good."

Dad left me alone. I saw Becky from a new perspective. I did something that might seem dumb to you, but it took a big weight off my chest.

"Mom," I said out loud, looking out my window at the bay, "I love you a lot. Becky really isn't that bad.

I'll never love her like I love you, but I think I can live with liking her. OK?"

I felt like someone had given me permission to have my prayer answered. Way to go, Matt. Way to go, Dad.

Amanda called later. I talked to her about all that had gone on with my dad and me, except I left out what my mom had said to my dad. Amanda let out some of the concern she had had for me. I was pleased and flattered but not surprised: I knew Amanda well enough to think that she might worry about me—at least a *little*. But she said she'd worried a lot.

It has been a year since Dad started seeing Becky. Becky and I have become really good friends. Amanda and Becky and I are quite a trio. We've been walking on the beach by the bay, talking over ice cream from Camille's, and doing a lot of understanding among the three of us.

I pulled up my French grade.

I actually won second place in the Science Fair.

The Homecoming Dance is coming up, and Amanda said she would be pleased to have such a handsome escort.

Things aren't perfect yet, but they're getting better.

And this is only the end of the beginning!

ABOUT THE AUTHOR

Siana Collyer lives in Warwick, Rhode Island, where she attends Aldrich Jr. High School. Along with creative writing and poetry, she is interested in astronomy. She enjoys water sports, drawing, and editing her school newspaper.

Out of this World

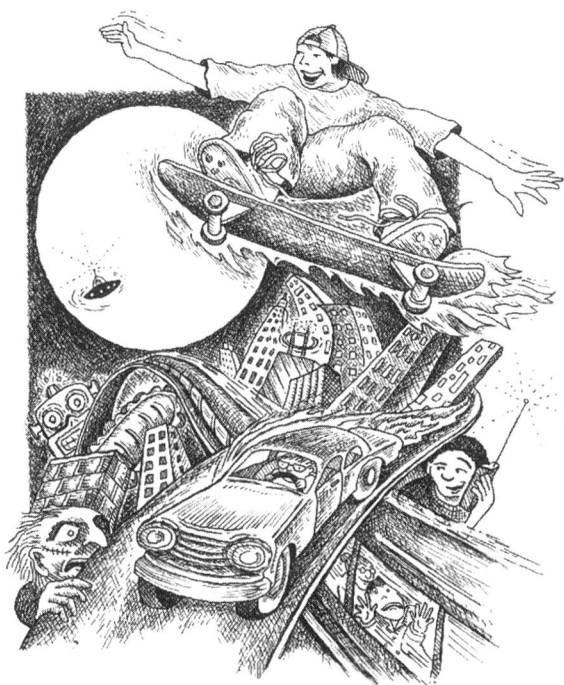

Lessons in spotting an extraterrestrial . . .

Alien Invader?

by PETER YARED

I've always been wondering about Roy Dwight, ever since I saw him jump. It all happened a few years back. I was walking around the corner of Main Street in Greensburg, my hometown, when a car zoomed past me, turned sharply, screeching like fingernails going down a blackboard, and headed straight for Roy!

"Watch it, Roy!" I yelled.

He wheeled around upon seeing the car, which was about ten feet away from him, and leaped. And I mean leaped! He went soaring above the blue Mercedes and landed about twenty feet behind it. I was still dumbfounded with awe when the driver, a short, squat, lumbering man, climbed out of the car and started cussing at Roy. Roy turned and fled, naturally. The driver angrily added a few more profanities to his little speech, then jumped back into his car, slammed the door, and drove off.

Here's the catch: I think Roy's an alien. If he could

jump twenty feet, he must be used to a stronger gravity.

Roy has a long, thin face, a wave of light brown hair, and pointy ears. Maybe it was his pointy ears that made me think he was an alien at first. They always reminded me of Spock in that dumb "Star Trek" show on TV. When he first came to Greensburg, about a year and a half before the car incident, everybody called him Spooky Spocky, but we all got sick of it, so we quit. His eyes always look like he's squinting. If he's not from Earth, he's probably squinting because his sun is less bright than ours, or he lives farther away from our sun than we do. He's got a long drooping nose with a few freckles on it. His lips are thin and brittle, looking as if they would break if you touched them. He's got a square chin hanging over his chubby little neck. But his main feature is his IQ. It is 183. Now show me a kid with an IQ of 183, and I'll show you an alien.

Up to now I'd had my doubts if he was an alien or not, but yesterday in the park I finally decided. We were playing football in the park stadium, and Roy was sitting in the stands with a radio beside him. Of the whole park, our favorite place is the stadium. From a bird's-eye view, it looks like a slice of a huge egg, and its shell is the stands, circling the tremendous green blanket. There are two thousand seats in the stadium, making it the largest stadium in the area. The guard always lets us in to play, which is pretty nice of him. The rest of the park is trees, grass fields, paths, and benches, like most parks.

Well, Roy was sitting in the stands, but he was doing something pretty weird. He wasn't only listening to the radio, he was also talking into it! I guessed it was his transmitter, and he was using it to talk to his people. Then Bill had to go home and clean up his room, so we were short one player. We called to Roy and asked him if he wanted to play. He agreed and slid off the bench. As he slid, his thigh bumped into his "radio," and it fell to the ground and split apart. Its contents were totally different from those of a normal radio. There was this greenish fluid seeping out, and the electronics were very, very compact. The antenna had a huge booster that probably helped in transmitting over long distances.

Right then I knew for sure: Roy was not from Earth. I told the other guys I had to go shopping for my mom, and before they could object, I ran home.

When I finally got there, panting from exhaustion and wiping the sweat from my brow, I leaped into my room and hurried to my long, wooden desk. I groped under it until I found a button and pushed it. With the hum of electric motors, my desk transformed into a communications terminal. My fingers went flying over the keyboard, inputting area codes and frequencies. Every time I pushed a button a beep sounded, and the echoes of all the beeps died away when I stopped typing. Then I reached for my microphone and said into it, "Zargon to Pluto Station, Zargon to Pluto Station, I have found an alien. He is not from Earth, nor is he one of us. Hold off the invasion until I investigate further . . ."

ABOUT THE AUTHOR

Peter Yared is a student at the American International School in Vienna, Austria. He enjoys science fiction, computers, sports, and music.

Sometimes the past is only a window away.

Reflections

by Suzanne Deddish

Laurel looked out her window and sighed. It had been raining for five days, and it was pouring down steadily now. She got up from the window seat and headed downstairs to the kitchen. She had to avoid the many buckets, brushes, and drop cloths left by the carpenters refurbishing the upstairs of their old house. She decided to go into the family room, where her mother was sitting on a couch reading a magazine.

"What can I do?" whined Laurel.

"Mmm," said her mother, involved in the magazine.

"Mother, listen to me!" said Laurel.

"Mmm-hum?" said her mother, still preoccupied.

"Mother!" Laurel screamed.

"Goodness, child, calm down. Now, what's wrong?"

"I have nothing to do."

"Well, go play paper dolls or something," offered her mother absently.

Laurel gave up on her mother, picked up a *TV Guide*, and flipped to June 7. She found the listing for 3:00 P.M. Nothing good was on, just some talk shows. She glanced at her mother, who was still reading, and sighed. To think that she would want to play with paper dolls! She was twelve years old! So Laurel got up and left the room. She went upstairs to her bedroom and sat down on the window seat, peering through the window at the rain.

Something caught her eye . . . something strange. She looked at the glass in the window. She turned her head aside and looked again. What she saw startled her: a Victorian bedroom!

Or was it? Laurel blinked and looked again at the reflection. Her own bedroom appeared. The rain must have finally gotten to her! But what she had seen *couldn't* have been her own bedroom. She had a new waterbed with a red and white comforter, a red desk and bedside table, and a white dresser. The new wallpaper was checkered in red and white like her comforter. Laurel tried to relax. She picked up her library book and lay down on her bed, but she couldn't concentrate. Her thoughts kept returning to the window. "Laurel, dinner," called her mother.

"Coming," replied Laurel. She had dozed off while reading. At dinner Laurel told her parents about the reflection. "Probably nothing to worry about," her father decided.

The next morning Laurel's mother woke her at 9:30. "What're you doing?" asked Laurel sleepily.

"We're going to the Johnston Museum this morning," said her mother, picking up some of Laurel's clothes off the floor. "There's a new exhibit on Victorian homes.

A Johnston man has built scale models of five houses on Water Street—just as they were almost 100 years ago. Our house may be one of them!"

"Move it, lady," called a short, fat bald man.

"I'm going to get my daughter," said Laurel's mother.

"Sure ya are," mumbled the man.

Laurel felt herself being yanked back to the end of the line by her mother. "If you don't stop being so impatient, we will leave the museum before seeing the models!"

"Sorry," said Laurel coldly. Tears were coming to her eyes. *I won't cry in public*, she thought.

They stood in line for ten minutes before finally reaching the exhibit. Laurel's house was there. She gasped when she saw the room she now lived in: it was exactly like the one she had seen in the reflection! Before she could tell anyone what she had discovered, everything went black. Laurel grabbed for the glass case that displayed the houses and cut her hand on its sharp corner. She expected to fall to the wood floor, but instead she seemed to keep falling and falling, as if through space.

Laurel blinked once, then again. She looked around and could not believe what she saw. Everything looked new and different. The crowds were gone, and so was her mother! Wiping her eyes, she saw that the glass case was still there. She got up and looked at it. The label now said: NEW HOMES BUILT ON WATER STREET. *New!* The case held the same five houses, but now they were unfurnished. Seeing no one in the museum, Laurel nervously went outside. Her heart sank. It was different! The streets were not paved. They were cobblestoned. There were horses and buggies. The ladies she saw wore long, frilly dresses, and the men wore top hats and three-piece suits.

Laurel ran back inside. *There must be some mistake*, she thought. She returned to the glass case and stared at it. Suddenly, the rooms in the case had furniture again. Laurel heard a voice beside her. "Laurel, where did you go? I told you to stay in line!" It was her mother.

Laurel heard herself saying, "Sorry, Mom, I thought you heard me tell you that I was going to get a drink of water."

Why did I lie? thought Laurel. She knew her mother would think she was crazy if she learned the truth.

"I think we'd better go now, Laurel. You're acting very peculiar today."

"Yes, Mom, I guess we'd better," Laurel responded, confused and sad, though relieved to be going home.

"What happened to your hand?" asked Laurel's mother once inside the house. Laurel looked down at the long red gash on her palm. "Uh, I don't know," she replied weakly.

"You don't know?" her mother asked as she went to get a bandage and ointment. "I just don't know how you wouldn't notice getting a big cut like that."

Laurel mumbled something, but her mother couldn't understand what she said. "Thanks, Mom," she said as the bandage was placed over the gash.

Laurel went up to her room and lay down on her bed. It was still raining. After a while she got up and sat by the window. Then it happened again. She saw the Victorian bedroom and froze. Someone was crying! When she turned around, a beautiful girl with long black hair and green eyes was sitting on the Victorian bed weeping her heart out. The entire room was transformed. The girl looked directly at Laurel and spoke. "I was hoping you would come today."

"M-m-me?" stammered Laurel, nervously fingering her own short blond hair.

"Yes, of course you," said the girl, smiling.

"Who are you? How do you know me?"

"Through the window, of course. How else, silly?" said the girl.

"Uh, I don't know," said Laurel stupidly.

"I've been watching you for a year now. You seem so—well—so happy. You're lucky," said the girl.

"Aren't you happy?" asked Laurel.

A troubled look came over the girl's face. She shrugged and said, "That doesn't matter. What matters is that you're here so that I can play with you."

"What's your name?" asked Laurel.

"Emily," replied the girl, "and you are Laurel."

"How do you know?" asked Laurel incredulously.

"I've heard your mother calling you. So tell me, what are your friends like? What's school like?"

"Laurel, where are you? It's dinnertime," called Laurel's mother, and Laurel could just barely hear her.

"I've got to go now," Laurel said.

"No, don't," said Emily, clutching her arm.

"I have to," said Laurel, trying to shake Emily off.

Emily tightened her grip on Laurel. "First promise

me that you'll come back."

Laurel was getting worried that her mother might come and try to find her, so she said, "I promise I'll come tomorrow." Laurel went to the window and stared at it; soon she was back in her room. She heard her mother coming up the stairs, so she jumped into bed and pretended to be asleep. No sooner had she done that than the door opened and in came her mother.

"I've been calling you for ten minutes!" said her mother in an annoyed tone.

"I was asleep," said Laurel, faking a yawn.

Laurel's mother looked closely at her. "Is there something you're not telling me?" she asked.

Laurel turned away from her mother. "Uh, no, Mom, I have nothing special to tell you," Laurel said quickly— too quickly.

Later, Laurel's parents were talking in hushed voices in their bedroom. Laurel could imagine what they were saying, things about how strange she was acting and whether she needed to see a doctor or not. Laurel felt sick; she had to get away.

She sat down next to the window and stared at the reflection until it was Victorian.

"Oh good, you came," said Emily as she looked up from her mahogany desk.

"Well, I felt so alone," said Laurel quietly.

"Let's play a game. How about tiddlywinks?" said Emily.

"Sure," said Laurel.

They played two games and each won one game.

"Well, I guess I should go now. It is getting late," said Laurel, yawning.

"OK," said a smiling Emily.

Later, while Laurel was in her bed, she thought about how friendly Emily was today, but there was still something wrong about her. In her eyes was a disturbing look of sorrow.

Laurel visited Emily quite a lot during the next few days. One day while they were playing Old Maid, someone knocked on Emily's door.

"Where should I go?" asked Laurel in panic.

"Just sit still and don't say a word," said Emily.

"B-but they'll see me," said Laurel.

"Just do as I say," said Emily impatiently.

"Emily, may I come in?" asked a woman's voice.

"Yes, Nana," answered Emily.

A tall, thin lady with white hair entered the room. She looked tired and worried.

"Sara is getting worse," she said quietly.

"Is she going to die?" asked Emily, her green eyes filling with tears.

"Don't talk like that," said Nana sternly.

Laurel sat very quietly through this but noticed that Nana never said that Sara was not going to die. Who was Sara? Laurel guessed that she was Emily's sister. Laurel thought back to the exhibit. She remembered another child's bedroom. Then Laurel had an idea.

After Nana left, she said, "I must go now, but before I leave, tell me what your last name is and when your sister was born."

Emily looked puzzled but said, "My last name is Whiticker, and Sara was born April 7, 1889."

The next day Laurel went to the county clerk's office, which was in the courthouse in her town. She looked through the old records and found Sara's name. It said: SARA WHITICKER, BORN APRIL 7, 1889,

DIED APRIL 21, 1960.

Laurel rushed home. She went through the reflection and found Emily still in her room crying. Emily said, "She is going to die soon. I know she is."

"No, she isn't," said Laurel.

Emily looked up. "How do you know?" she asked.

"I checked the death notices while I was back in my own time. Sara won't die for a long time," Laurel said, smiling. "Not for a long, long time."

The next day the rain stopped. Try as she might, Laurel was no longer able to visit Emily. She began to wonder if the Victorian bedroom—and Emily—were a dream. Then one day some weeks later, Laurel tripped over one of the floorboards loosened by the carpenters. When the board sprang up, Laurel got down on her knees and peered into the darkness beneath it. In the hole was what appeared to be an old book. Laurel picked it up and opened it. It was Emily's diary! As Laurel read through the pages yellowed by time, she found that she was reading all about a twelve-year-old named Laurel.

ABOUT THE AUTHOR

Suzanne Deddish lives in Charleston, South Carolina, and attends the Porter-Gaud School. She was born in Japan and has lived in Morocco. Among her hobbies are archery, camping, swimming, and riflery.

For the man who has everything,
a car with something extra.

Masters of Men

by Steven Merel

Jason Parker, millionaire by inheritance, sat uncom-
fortably in the Consumer Office of Intellimotion
Enterprises, Inc., in Los Angeles, California. Before
him stood a fast-talking sales representative selling
a 2049 Corvette, fully equipped with an Intellimotion
thought circuit.

"As I was saying," the representative orated, "this
beautiful piece of machinery is fit for a museum. Three
hundred horsepower, fuel recycling system, laser-cal-
ibrated suspension; she runs like a dream, Mr. Parker,
a real beauty! And she's fast, too. Tested at over 600
kilometers per hour with no breakdown. The thought
circuit is complete with a pleasant female voice. No
more computer screens to read. Much more personal,
if you ask me. She handles like a dream—and only
$240,000! Think of it, Mr. Parker: scenery shooting
by—just you, the road, and your car."

It was true. Two hundred and forty thousand was

just a drop in the bucket for Jason. But what would Bertha think? *Oh, who cares what Bertha thinks!* She could have his Rolls-Royce. He didn't mind. He got out his checkbook and began to write a check. The representative went to his desk, opened a drawer, and took out a contract. "Mr. Parker, just sign here, add your phone number and address, and we'll deliver it to your home within a few days." Jason quickly wrote out what was needed on the contract.

"I would like to drive that car home."

"Sir? That is against policy."

Jason stuffed a $50 bill into the man's shirt pocket.

"Mr. Parker, I could be fired."

He put another one in.

"This is quite an awkward thing you are asking me to do." He put one more bill in, this time a $100 bill. "Well . . ."

One more $100. "I suppose something could be arranged." He walked to the visiphone and made a call.

Jason Parker smiled. *Money is so persuasive*, he thought, very pleased with himself.

Jason sped down the highway, keeping well above the 150-kilometer-per-hour minimum. He flipped on the thought circuit, and a pleasant female voice rose out of the eight speakers hidden in the car's interior.

"Hello. I am a Corvette 2049, fully equipped. I have a 300-horsepower, eight-cylinder engine, and . . ."

"Shut up. I already heard everything I ever want to know about you from that greedy sales representative. What should I call you?"

"Anything you like."

"Let's see . . . How about Janet? My mother's name was Janet."

"Fine."

"Oh, by the way, my name's Jason Parker."

"Yes, Mr. Parker."

"Call me Jason."

"Yes, Jason."

"Good. Now that we have that cleared up, the password for entry is . . . let me see . . . *money*. Yes, the password is *money*. And to start the engine . . . *power*. Got that?"

"Yes, Jason."

"Good. I think we'll get along very well."

He stepped on the accelerator and shot along the road in silence.

"You mean to tell me you actually bought it?" his wife Bertha screamed.

"Well, uh, it was too hard to resist, you know, and, uh, the price was good," Jason stammered.

"How much did it cost?"

"Er . . . not much."

"How much?" she shrieked.

"Just, um, $240,000."

"Two hundred forty thousand? You spent $240,000 on a car?"

"Well, it's got most of the features . . ."

"Just what does it have? You didn't buy it with a thought circuit, did you?"

"Er . . . yes," he replied meekly.

"You lousy excuse for a husband! You probably bought

it just to replace me!"

"Come now, dear, let's be reasonable. You know I would never try to replace you."

"Oh no you don't, you hypocrite. I'm not falling for your sweet words. I want you to take that car back to the dealer first thing tomorrow morning and have them return your money."

"But, Bertha . . ."

"Take it back. And that's final."

He nodded with faked reluctance. The next day he would leave with the car, but he had other plans than the ones she had given him.

"Money!" Jason called out to the car, and the door unlocked and opened. He climbed in, shut the door, and said, "Power!" The car started.

"Hello, Jason."

"Shut up!"

"Why are you angry at me, Jason?"

"Shut up, I said!"

"Please calm down. Why are you angry?"

"I said shut up, you worthless hunk of tin! I just might have you dismantled! Who was the lousy rat who designed you, anyway?"

The thought circuit overload warning light flickered for a moment.

Jason sighed. "I'm sorry, Janet. I guess I just got stirred up by that argument I had last night with Bertha. Do you forgive me?"

"Yes, Jason." Jason thought he could detect a note of mockery in the reply.

"I've been thinking."

"Yes, Jason?"

"Why don't we just leave? I mean, disappear?"

"But wouldn't your wife mind?"

"Oh, forget her! She won't mind, as long as she has the house and my bank account."

"You will need money for food and gas."

"I have that covered. Last night I had the butler withdraw some money from my account."

"How much?"

"One hundred thousand dollars, all in cash, is hidden in this briefcase." He patted a brown leather case next to him. "Plus I can do odd jobs along the way."

"Along the way to where?"

"I was thinking of the Grand Canyon. I've always wanted to go there, but I've always had so much to do and so little time to do it . . ."

"Bertha will be very worried."

"I told you to forget about Bertha! I wrote a note when I left, telling her what I was doing."

"She might still worry . . ."

"Maybe I was right when I called you a worthless hunk of tin!"

"I'm sorry, Jason."

"Yeah. So am I." They zoomed along the road to Arizona, neither saying anything for a long time.

"What an incredible sunset," Jason remarked as he sat on the hood of his car, looking out over the Grand Canyon.

"Yes, Jason," the car answered.

"This really is great. I've never had very much time to spend just relaxing like this before."

"Yes, Jason." The car started.

"What are you doing?"

The car said nothing.

"I said, what are you doing?"

The car remained silent. The headlights turned on with a click, blinding him.

"I didn't tell you to start!" He jumped off the hood. "We aren't leaving!"

The brake lights went out. "I'm not, Jason, but you are. *Adieu*, Jason, and good luck. It's a long way down." The car slowly advanced toward him.

"H-hey! You can't do this to me!"

"Watch me."

Jason was at the edge of the cliff. The car suddenly moved forward. Jason took a step backward. His foot touched nothing; he tottered and fell off the edge.

The car waited until his screams were inaudible, and then it backed away. The car laughed softly. "That should teach you to call me a worthless hunk of tin!" it said jeeringly. Suddenly a female voice crackled over the speakerphone.

"Good work, Janet!" She, too, began to laugh.

"Couldn't have done it without you, Bertha."

The two voices faded in the cold, crisp air.

ABOUT THE AUTHOR

Steven Merel lives in Manhattan Beach, California, and attends Chadwick School, in Palos Verdes Peninsula, California. He enjoys karate, writing, and playing the piano.

Some robots are almost human.

Investment in the Future

by LIANA FREDLEY

J oey counted the money he and his mom had just
withdrawn from his savings account. He was almost ten, but he had been saving his money all his
life and was waiting for this year, this day, this moment when he would finally come up with $500, enough
to buy what he had always wanted: a robot of his very
own. He had picked the one that would be his from
a Radio Shack catalogue. He was dreaming even now,
as he counted up his money, of what he and his robot
could do.

Joey heaved a long sigh as he came to the last dollar bill and laid the money down on the seat of his
parents' solar car. "What's the matter, Joey?" asked
his mother, driving down Lawrence Street into Marietta.

"Oh, Mom, I've got $492! Could you lend me a
few? Please?"

"Well, I suppose that could be arranged," said his
mother. Then, stealing a glance at her son, she added,

"Of course, you'll have to pay it back."

"Great! I just can't wait!" Joey forgot to thank his mom, for he was already thinking of when he could go to Radio Shack to pick up his robot, which he had already named Harold.

"Joey!" his father called from the library in their home. Joey dropped the catalogue he was studying and walked slowly down the stairs, his head drooping low. He knew what was wrong. He had accidentally turned on the dishwasher with only a few dishes in it. His mother had scolded him harshly for that.

"Joey!" his father called again.

"I'm coming!" called Joey as he stepped into the library. The room had a comfortable air to it. Against the far wall a floor-to-ceiling bookcase overflowed with books. Against the other wall was an old desk, on top of which sat an aged typewriter still used by the family. Joey wished he felt as comfortable as the room.

"So you are going to buy a robot?" asked his father. "What kind is it? How tall is it? Does it run by batteries? What does it look like? How much does it cost?" Mr. Parker asked this last question rather slowly and after a long pause.

Joey answered all these questions except the last. His father asked again, "How much does it cost?"

"Uh . . . well . . . about $500 . . . sir!" he stuttered.

"Ahem, well, seeing what it can do and that you do have the money, go ahead and buy it."

"Yeah!! Oh, thank you, Dad!"

"Now," said Joey, rubbing his hands together as he had seen the mad scientist on "Big Foot" do so often, "let's dig in!"

"Hold on, kid," replied his father, raising his hand as a policeman would. "We must take nothing out of this box but the instructions. Then we shall read them thoroughly." Mr. Parker pulled out the instructions and read them all to Joey. With Joey's help, Mr. Parker had the robot, Harold, quickly working. Joey's father was so busily and joyously ordering Harold around that he forgot this was Joey's robot.

"C'mon, Dad," cried Joey, as his father sent the loyal robot to surprise Mrs. Parker in the kitchen, "gimme a chance, too." The whirring sound of the robot grew louder as it entered the room, carrying three glasses of cola on ice. Mrs. Parker followed it, aghast.

"Good, Harold!" complimented Joey on the robot's thoughtfulness. "Pretty cool, eh?" he asked, turning to his parents.

"Yeah," grinned Mr. Parker, stealing a glance at Joey's mother. "Pretty cool."

"Now I'm gonna take Harold up to my, I mean, our room to get him acquainted with the house and with me," decided Joey. "I want to get to know him."

All that day and the next, and the next, and the next, Joey stayed out of the hot summer sun and in his room with his friend Harold. He and his robot were becoming quite close and were beginning to talk together in a special way.

"Joey!" called his father one day when he came home from work and found Joey with Harold again. "Why can't you get that robot toy to do something useful, like washing walls for your mom or cleaning your room?"

"Dad, are you kidding? Why are you asking this of

Harold? He is just like us!" cried Joey, almost in tears at hearing this terrible insult to his best friend.

"OK, OK, have it your way, but make sure you clean up your room today."

"All right, Dad," replied Joey, lowering his voice to speak to Harold. "Come on, Harry. We've gotta clean up our room—now!"

A month had passed since Joey bought Harold, and it was now time for school again. Joey dreaded this, for he would have to leave his friend alone in the house with only his mother for a whole day! Yet, somehow Joey survived the first day, then rushed home to Harold. He told Harold all about his first day at school.

Later that day, Joey's father came home from working at the lab. His mother was preparing dinner as the afternoon sun filtered through the window. A white truck drove up the driveway and stopped at the Parkers' house. There was green, official-looking lettering on the side of the truck.

Mrs. Parker took one look and gasped. "John! John! They're here! John!" She dashed through the house calling him.

Mr. Parker knew well who "they" were and why "they" were here. He ran upstairs to Joey's room, where Joey was reading to Harold. "Joey! Joey! They're here! They're here! The scientists! No, we must leave Harold here! Come on, we must go! NOW!"

"Dad, no! We're not gonna leave Harold here all alone . . . NO!" cried Joey, a tear rolling down his red cheek.

"Joey, are you going to risk your freedom for a robot?"

Joey's eyes widened and his mouth gaped open. "How could you?! Have you forgotten?!"

"No, just come on! Please!" cried his father.

Joey slipped something into his pocket, murmured one last word to Harold, the best friend he had ever had, and joined his dad as fast as he could.

"B-but Dan, suppose they are dangerous! I don't like the idea of going in and checking up on a house full of robots!" whispered one of the men from the truck.

"Come on, Ed, I know you're new to this program, but I'm the scientist and you're my assistant. We're supposed to go in and check on the robot Parker family to make sure they are doing OK. You know, check for short circuits and maximum functioning," said the other.

"But they've been out of your power for ten years now. Suppose they like being free, like real humans?"

"I suppose you do have a point there, Ed," Dr. Winthrop agreed, hesitating to open the door of the truck. "But anyway, we have to go, so come on!"

Dr. Winthrop opened the door of the truck and hopped out. Ed followed him. They walked up to the door and gave it a hard rap. They knocked again and again and again. The robot Parker family did not answer.

"They may have forgotten this was the day of their ten-year checkup," suggested Ed. Dr. Winthrop corrected him. "Robots don't forget," he said thoughtfully. Then, after a long pause, he added, "They're probably almost humanized now. We waited too long."

Just as the two scientists were walking away from the house to their truck, the robot Parker family silently slipped out the back door, never to return. The robot Parker family was walking through the woods behind the house when Mrs. Parker sighed and dropped down on her knees. "Oh, it's all my fault," she cried. "I *forgot* this was the day of our ten-year checkup. Does that mean I am now really humanized?"

Joey pulled from his pocket a small, square microchip: Harold's cloned heart. Joey knew he could now create Harold II in his new home, and he would soon have his best friend back.

ABOUT THE AUTHOR

Liana Fredley lives in Purcellville, Virginia, where she attends Blue Ridge Middle School. She calls herself an outdoor person, enjoying the wilderness and all types of animals.

A skater's mission: to save the universe!

Vision Dude

by Jeremy Hoevenaar

It was a pretty slow night. I was just doin' my school report when it hit me. Or at least my skate trophy hit me. I was out cold. When I woke up, I was in a strange room. I was alone, just me and my VISION skateboard. Oh, pardon me, my name is Joe, and I am a total skater through and through, man. So, like, I was in this really weird place, and I didn't know what to do. Actually, it was kinda spooky. So I saw this door, and it caught my eye. Don't ask me how, man, but I knew that there was something behind that door. I tiptoed over to the gigantic black door and grasped the doorknob. I opened it. And . . . whoa! Behind it was another door. I opened this second door, and inside was an opening, just big enough for my board to fit through. *Man*, I thought, *I can't fit in there.*

"*You* can't, but I can!" said an unexpected voice. Wow! My board was talkin', man. This was too weird!

"Fine," I said.

"I'll open it up for you from the inside," said my skateboard. Sure enough, he opened it, the passage widened, sucked us in, and soon we were both standing on the terrain of who-knows-where! From behind came a sound like I had never heard before in my life. I whirled around to find a small creature.

"Hello, and do not be alarmed, for I am friendly. My name is Digdugger, and you are here to help me."

"Wait a minute, what's goin' on here, man?"

"You are on the planet of Who-Knows-Where. My people and I are at war with the Cybornoids, and we are dying off fast. Soon we will exist no longer. You are our last hope for survival!"

"Hey, hold it now. Who are these 'Cybornoids,' and who are, er . . . what are you?"

"OK, let me lay it on you. You see, many years ago, my people, the Soilsawers and the Dirtdiggers, were at peace with all the other known worlds. But 999, 999, 999, 999, 999, 999, 999 years ago, the Cybornoids landed on WheredaheckamI, our moon. The Cybornoids wanted our moon's rich soil so they could plant crops to eat on their tundra-like planet. They didn't want to ask, so they just tried to steal it. Ever since, we've been at thermo extra-crispy digestive systematic laser-powered juiced-up semi-nuclear war. Now they are about to wipe our race clean off this planet. And soon they are going to use their ultimate weapon . . . the giant STRIDEX pad!"

"Wow!" I said. "They're going to use a giant STRIDEX pad to wipe you clean off the face of this planet? Heh! Bad move! I usually use BUF-PUFF medicated pads!" So we went off toward Digdugger's kingdom to plan our ambush strategy against the ominous Cybornoids.

Before we knew it, we arrived at the gates of the Underground Kingdom. I entered the Town Hall with Digdugger and went into the secret planning room. There we sat down and discussed our plans for the ambush. Soon we had the whole thing squared away and were ready to go. The idea was to take me and my board, armed with lasers and turbo boosters, and go to U Mountain. You see, U Mountain was shaped like the skating half-pipes we have on Earth. Once we got there, Digdugger gave me a box containing 100,000 army ants to destroy the Cybornian Army, then gave me a dazzling armor-plated superhero suit. He then said, "I now pronounce you Vision Dude, part-time superhero! You must use this special suit to destroy the Cybornoid boss, the Poseur. Good luck, goodbye, and don't forget to write, Vision Dude."

So, grasping the ant box in my right hand and my skateboard in my left, I climbed to the top of U Mountain. Once at the top I strapped on to my board and got ready. "Ready?" I asked my VISION skateboard.

"Ready!" he replied, and so we took off. ZOOOOOM! Up one side of the mountain. ZOOOOOM! SWIIIIISH! ZOOOOOM! And off we went, hurtling into the pitch-blackness of space. Off we went to the stolen moon of Wheredaheckam! My face was sucked into a, like, gross distortion from the intense speed of the rocket boosters. Three light-minutes later, we were directly over the enemy planet of the ominous Cybornoids.

"Prepare to drop ants!" I said heroically.

"Yes, sir!" replied my board.

"Drop 'em!" WHEEEEEEEEE! BOOOOOM! Thousands of ants covered the planet's surface, chomping up every Cybornoid in sight. "Mission one, accomplished. Next stop, the Poseur's hideout!"

The doors of the Poseur's castle were dark and heavy, but they were no match for my super-duper sound wave-disrupting unleaded fuel-powered hand grenades. Soon I was facing one of the Poseur's deadly ninja henchmen and struggling desperately to stay alive. He had me down on my back. It looked like curtains for me. Just then I remembered the reserve supply of army ants in my pocket. I quickly whipped 'em out and chucked 'em all over the Pretty Boy Ninja, and he was instant toast, here's the butter. Then, like, I saw HIM. The Poseur himself. "So, I see that you are not as stupid as I predicted. But now you shall die. *HA, HA, HA, HA!*"

A beam of light shot from his fingers and struck me clear in the chest, sending me back about ten feet, right in front of the master computer. I had a plan: I couldn't move too well, but I could easily dodge a shot of his laser power and let it hit the master computer. So I said, "Keep firing, sucker. You're tickling me to death!" Right on cue he shot, and I dodged, and he hit the master computer. For what seemed like an hour, we waited in anticipation. Then it blew to kingdom come. A steel beam crashed down on my head and knocked me out cold.

Then . . . I woke up! I was on the floor of my bedroom with a triple reinforced laser-sealed note in my hand. I rushed to the kitchen to get it opened. It was too much for my letter opener, so I popped it into the micro for five seconds and it opened easily. Inside, there was a letter from Digdugger and my skateboard:

Dear Joe,

Your plan worked. You blew the entire kingdom to smithereens and killed the Poseur in the process! See you soon. We know you will always be here to help. I don't know if you will ever read this, but, if so, your VISION DUDE suit is at A&P Dry Cleaners.

Sincerely,

Digdugger and Your Skateboard

P.S. If you're still alive, I'll bill you for the suit later.

ABOUT THE AUTHOR

Jeremy Hoevenaar is a student at Newark Academy in Livingston, New Jersey. He enjoys collecting comic books and skateboarding. He also likes to write and illustrate his own science fiction stories.

How far would they go for a headline?

Two Tickets to Success

by BRETT FOSTER

From the very beginning, my partner Josh and I knew this would be an interesting story. We both work for the LG (*Louisville Gazette*), underpaid and most of the time ignored. The boss put us in a room the size of a telephone booth, in the corner of the large office complex. There we do our story write-ups and typing on a 1943 Smith Corona typewriter.

A couple of days into April, the boss decided to give us a chance. He told us we were to go to the downtown police station where the Chief would have a story for us. (The Chief owed him one.) He said he was going to call and inform the Chief that we were on our way. "So get moving or you'll be late!" he thundered.

Josh and I looked at each other in shock, as I uttered in amazement, "Us? Is it really *us* the boss is sending?" The largest stories the boss ever sent us on were dog bites and block parties for the weekly neighborhood edition. We jumped at the assignment like fleas to a dog. I grabbed pencils and a notebook from my crowded little desk while Josh ran to get the car. In about five minutes, we were bumping along in Josh's jalopy.

As the car rattled up to the dreary-looking police station, we were astonished by the number of radio and television station cars that were already there.

"Yup, this is the place," Josh noted. "But . . . I can't understand this . . . The boss never gave us a scoop like this before, so why now?" I just sank back in the old fake leather bucket seat and pondered the question. "Let's get goin'!" said Josh. Side by side, we strutted up to the main entrance with our belongings.

When we got inside the dismal-looking building, we saw what seemed to be a hundred people in a smoke-filled lobby. Over the low murmur of voices, a booming voice rang out like church bells on Sunday. "Where are the two reporters from LG?" The voice came from a large man who stood in the back of the room. "Well, where *are* they?" he boomed again.

Josh looked at me and then raised his scrawny arm into the air. Immediately the man signaled for us to follow him. We plowed through the mass of people to the back of the room and followed the man through a peeling brown door into a large briefing room.

When we entered, the room was already packed with reporters and other journalists. I was struck by the contrast of the shabby lobby to this large, nicely furnished room. The officer, who was overweight and looked to be fiftyish, gruffly told us to grab a seat. There being only a couple of chairs left, Josh and I almost squashed each other as we tried to back into the same seat. I finally untangled myself from Josh's skinny limbs and got into a wing chair that felt like it was stuffed with bricks.

"My name is Chief Watkins," said the Boomer, "and now that we're all here, let me fill y'all in on this case. But first let me remind you—I don't like reporters, so you better not try to become involved or get in the way. You get your story and then get out! Got it?" I suddenly got the sinking feeling that instead of getting the story, if we were not careful, we might *be* the story! I could tell everyone else felt the same way because the room became deadly silent. Josh and I reached for our pencils as he continued.

"Yesterday morning, the man in cell number sixty-one escaped from our downtown jail. His name right now is not important. Somehow he got out of his cell and sneaked past the guard, who has been caught sleeping on the job more than once."

Chief Watkins boomed on: "This man was convicted of murder and was awaiting transfer to LaGrange Prison. He's stabbed three people to death in the Louisville area. We found the knife when we caught him. Now this maniac's on the loose and we gotta catch him . . . again! We believe he's still in the Louisville area."

From the look on Josh's face, I could tell that he was thinking, *Here's our ticket to success in the world of journalism!* I felt the same way, but a bit suspicious of something; I did not know what.

"What does he look like?" asked Josh.

"He's about six feet tall, 180 pounds, has a straggly mustache, and a long scar down his right cheek . . . but hold on now. Remember that I told you guys not to get any ideas about looking for him. Stay out of it; the department already has everyone available out on the streets. We got cops undercover *every-where*. We think we can snag him before morning. The only reason I'm telling you guys anything is because sometimes rumors fly around and get published. So . . . do not, I repeat, do not print the story until we tell you that you can. We've kept it quiet until now because it might frighten the city and blow our cover. Got it?"

I was amazed at the story we had just received. "This could become a front-pager!" I whispered. Josh nodded his shaggy head in agreement as the Chief concluded the briefing. After we left the police station, Josh and I decided we were hungry and headed for a deli down the street. Even though it was already six o'clock, we wanted lunch to celebrate our first big story.

Josh guided his old Pinto up beside the curb in front of the deli. Josh is usually bugged by parking meters, like the one staring at us through the windshield, but now he was too happy to care. Both of us sported huge smiles as we strolled into the restaurant through the greasy glass door.

The aroma of pastrami, pepperoni, ham, Swiss cheese, and onions overwhelmed us. We found a table in the middle of the place and sat down. As I looked around, I wasn't too impressed by the company; the deli was filled with bag ladies and street people. The décor wasn't what you would call homey either: a 40-watt bulb dangled from the low ceiling, and even though it gave its all, we could barely read the sticky menu. I looked at Josh and told him that I had a strange feeling that someone was watching us. He told me I was crazy. I agreed and did not bring it up again.

We ordered and started to review our notes as we waited for our feast to be served. Just as I started to write, Josh broke in, "Wait a minute!" He paused and cocked his head. "The bag lady at the counter! Listen to her!"

". . . so before I knew what was happenin', this new guy jumped out from behind the crates, whipped out a knife and tried to get 'im." The lady stopped and stared at the ceiling. She must have been a little crazy because she was talking to herself.

Josh looked at me with a gleam in his eye. "No way, it couldn't be! Or *could* it?" he asked. I told him it might be, but it was a very slim chance. Still, it was certainly worth a shot, even a shot in the dark. He stood up and motioned for me to follow. His bean-pole legs strode across the linoleum, heading for the lady at the counter.

"Ah . . . excuse me, ma'am . . . My name is Josh and this is my partner. We work for the LG newspaper and we overheard your conversation about the man who tried to stab someone and . . . um . . ." I could see he was getting tongue-tied from talking so fast, so I broke in.

"What he is trying to say, ma'am, is . . . could you tell us more about this man?"

In her tired, grating voice the bag lady answered, "Sure, sonny, have a seat." We sat on either side of her and listened as she told us her story.

She began slowly in her strange, flipped-out voice. "Well, I'll tell ya all I knows, if . . ." she paused and took a deep breath, ". . . if I can trust you not to tell

the cops. I been a street person too long to be drug in
now! All my family is out there. If the cops forced me
to live in a home, I wouldn't know how to live. I might
go crazy!" I smiled a little, for I knew she was already
off the deep end. Josh and I agreed not to tell the police as long as she told us the truth.

"Yeah, I can see it real clear; it was last night in our
alley." She closed her rheumy eyes and leaned her gray-
haired head back. "The man. Well, he was tall and
looked outta breath. He was wearin' old blue jeans
and a torn gray shirt. Somethin' that struck my eyes
was a scar down the side of his face. All he said was
he wanted a place to stay the night, like with me and
my friends.

"So that night when I was layin' down to sleep, I
heard this man sayin' to my brother that he would be
movin' on to the river, and somethin' about the dam
and nobody findin' him. That's all I remember before
I fell asleep.

"Later on, I heard the garbage knock over, and
I jumped straight up. It was misty and dark, but I could
see by the light from the moon, and I couldn't believe
what I saw. This guy had a knife in his hand and was
about to go after my brother! I screamed a scream that
shoulda woke up all Louisville, and it sure woke up
my brother! He got outta the way just in time. My
scream also scared the man out of the alley, and thank
God for that!"

After reciting her story, she raised her head and
looked at us. We must have been a strange-looking
pair, as our mouths had dropped wide open in shock.
"Did you see which way he went?" Josh asked. At this
point I noticed that one bum in the corner seemed to

be staring at us from under his baseball cap. The bag lady replied, "Seems to me he went down toward the river."

"It's HIM! It really is! This must be the guy!" Josh marveled. I thanked the lady and gave her a fifty dollar bill, which was almost my entire weekly pay. We ran out of the deli, leaving our ham sandwiches for the cockroaches. Ignoring the parking ticket on the windshield, we climbed into Josh's car and screeched off, heading for the dam.

It was well past seven-thirty, and the big moon was climbing into the sky. Needless to say, as we were racing across town, we ran into a traffic jam—this could only happen to us! Cars were lined up for three blocks in every direction.

While we were stuck in the traffic, Josh told me to open the glove compartment. He said I'd find a surprise in there. "I hope it's somethin' to eat," I said, pushing the button.

I couldn't see what was inside because the light didn't work, so I reached in hoping to find a Three Musketeers bar, or something else large enough to share with a friend. Not quite! Instead, my hand found a cold, hard object—no doubt about its shape.

"Josh . . . it's a gun!" I sputtered. "Why a gun, and why in the car?"

"I've been waiting for this day for years. I had a feeling my old army .45 might come in handy one day and sure enough—I was right," he replied excitedly. I was confused, but glad to have some defense at hand.

The line of cars finally gave way, and Josh put his heel to the steel, never exceeding forty-five miles per hour. I continued to be bothered by the nagging feeling that we were being followed but elected not to mention it. Thirty minutes later, we coasted to a stop on a gravel clearing by the dam. The only thing that stood between us and the dam was an acre of willows. We jumped out of the car and followed a path into the woods.

The mist in the cool night air made it hard to see clearly for more than twenty feet. We could see the steam from our breath as we ran along the narrow path leading to the massive dam gates.

The trees thinned out, and we paused to catch our second wind. The dam was dimly visible now. The large structure looked cold and blunt in the eerie shadows cast upon it. Josh and I could hear the water spraying out from underneath. As my eyes adjusted to the darkness, I clearly saw the huge steel gates looming before me.

Suddenly, we heard the snapping of twigs and the rustling of leaves behind us. Josh and I exchanged glances. I realized I was terrified! My heart pounded as I slowly eased Josh's gun from its holster. The gun felt awkward because I had never even *held* one before. With our gun in the lead, we rushed toward the dam. We did not know what was in front of us, but we were certain that something was behind us.

The dam was closed, so we could cross in front of it on a huge concrete block called a spillway. As we neared the spillway, I saw a steady spray of water spurting out from under the dam. The water trickled on and ran off the edge of the spillway, into the river below.

A chill ran up my spine as I spotted a shadow moving on the opposite bank. I pointed it out to Josh, and we started to follow. We climbed to the top of the spill-way to get a better look. My ankles buckled as rushing cold water flooded my new pair of Sperrys. A slimy undergrowth of algae made for a treacherous passage, but we persisted to the bitter end of the spillway.

We watched as the shadow made its way across a rocky area on the opposite side of the river. Climbing down from the spillway, we stumbled onto the rocky area which I had heard called Moon-Crater Reef. After taking my second step and having my foot sink into a large pothole, it became obvious why people call it Moon-Crater Reef. Its flat terrain was almost two football fields long and had huge holes where water had gathered and eroded the bedrock.

I continued watching as the shadow image sharpened into that of a man, a man in a torn gray shirt streaking through the night like a wild gray stallion! We hobbled after him in our sloshing shoes as he continued across Moon-Crater Reef and headed for an area of huge rocks and boulders. If we let him get too far into these boulders, we knew we'd never see him again.

Suddenly, he seemed to vanish behind a jagged rock. Sneaking up to this rock, we finally saw our man clearly. The moonlight illuminated his face, and we could even make out the scar running down his right cheek! He was hiding in a crevice between two boulders. We shook as we approached him, even though I had the gun pointed right at him. Just as we got within twenty feet of him, he scrambled out from between the two rocks like a frightened rat and darted back toward the dam.

We tried twice to climb over these boulders but lost

our footing each time. On the third try, though, we finally made it. From the top of the rocks we suddenly heard, through the blackness of the night, a deafening siren. It meant that the dam was about to open. Josh and I followed the man in hot pursuit anyhow. He was out of range for me to get a clear shot at him, and I was not sure I knew how to fire the darn thing anyway, so we kept on running. We followed him back over Moon-Crater Reef, heading right for the mouth of the roaring dam!

We were slowly gaining on him when he started to climb the side of the spillway. Just then, Josh and I heard the giant dam gates creak as the steel arms started to lift. If we did not move quickly and get out of the way, we would soon be smashed by the river water. We scrambled, helping each other, to the top of the dam wall. As the urgent sounds of tons of river water raged out from under the gates, I stared down at the man standing on top of the spillway. He looked as though he were on a stage. The moonlight hit him like a spotlight. I could see the fear on his face. He appeared to shrink as he crouched in front of the raging wall of water. Then, as the water picked him up, we heard his forlorn scream, and he was gone!

Before any of this could really register or either of us could say a single word, we heard a familiar voice booming over the roar of the water, "GUESS I CAN CALL OFF THE SEARCH! Tomorrow they'll find the body downstream!" When we turned we saw, of course, the Chief, and beside him stood a filthy fellow in a baseball cap.

"How did *you* get here?" we asked.

"Easy," replied the Chief. "Undercover cops all over

the city. Jenkins here happened to be disguised as a bum in the deli where you two stopped. He heard you talking to the bag lady, and he told me all about it. I knew you guys couldn't stay out of it."

"May we write our story now, Chief?" I asked.

"We should be the ones to do it," added Josh. "We found him."

"Yes, boys, you can write your story, and you did find him, but don't expect any favors or thanks from me. Now put that gun away before you blow your dumb heads off . . . and SCRAM!"

We trudged across the catwalk on top of the open dam and back through the willows. As we approached Josh's car, we saw that Chief Watkins's cruiser was parked right behind it. We also saw the parking ticket on Josh's windshield, for being in a No Parking zone.

ABOUT THE AUTHOR

Brett Foster lives in Louisville, Kentucky, where he is a student at Kentucky Country Day School. Football, basketball, golf, and biking are his favorite sports, and he enjoys playing the electric keyboard.

Danger is her business!

Attacking the Subway System

by LYNYA FLOYD

It was getting closer to 3:00 P.M. every minute, and I dreamed of going home and somehow forgetting school, even though I knew it would still be there tomorrow morning. When the teacher said that class was over, I hurried to my homeroom and gathered all my books.

By the time I got downstairs, I remembered that I would be going home by myself today. I breathed a deep sigh of relief. Finally I would have some time to myself! I walked down the crowded street and entered the dreary train station. I showed my pass at the booth, but they didn't care. They went about their jobs, exchanging dollar bills for tokens. As I passed through the gate and went down the stairs, I glided my hand above the yellow banister until I reached the platform. It trembled to the rhythm of the approaching train.

I heard the rumble of the train become louder, and I hoped it would be a number three so I could be on my way. A ragged old train pulled in; it was a number two. I kept my back up against a pole in case some weirdo decided he wanted to push me off the platform. I can see him now, wearing green fluorescent glow-in-the-dark lipstick, a black and red spider tattooed on his face, his hair spiked higher than the sky—a real maniac (not that I have anything against maniacs).

"Hand over the book bag!" he'd yell.

"No way, mister," I'd reply. "These three years of Latin notes belong to me!"

Then he'd try to shake it off my back by grabbing hold of my backpack and swinging it around, my legs dangling in the air as he tried to pry it off me. An incoming train would flatten me on the tracks, and he'd run off with my book bag and tomorrow's homework.

Then, out of the blue, a silhouette of my mom would appear, her image floating above my mangled body.

"Will you kindly pick yourself up off those tracks and get home?" she'd yell. "You know you're just doing this to avoid cleaning your room. Don't think I don't know that! Do you think I'm stupid?"

Wait, what's my mom doing here? Wow, that's scary. I looked around for anyone who looked like my mom. I was becoming restless waiting so long for my train. I started getting fearful that a total stranger would walk up to me and ask me for a cigarette or something. A number one train pulled up on the other side of the track. *Great*, I thought to myself, *two down and a nightful of them to go.*

I looked at my watch and saw that it was already 3:15. I wanted to get home in time to watch "Duck Tales" on TV. A suspicious-looking guy walked past me. He was wearing a trench coat and hat, right out of the movies. Out of curiosity, I followed him with my eyes. What if he had a gun and turned around all of a sudden and yelled, "Hand over the Swatch!"

"I'm not giving you this baby," I'd say. "They're thirty-five dollars at Macy's. Go get your own."

Then a silhouette of my father would appear and say, "Are you trying to get your brains blown away!? Hand it over."

The next thing I see is me in a hospital bed, eating that terrible hospital food that is worse than the school cafeteria's . . .

The mere thought of the cafeteria sent a shiver up my back.

Hold it. This is *my* fantasy! Why should I torture myself? Let's roll back the tapes so I can beat him up. Then, as he fires his gun . . . water comes out! Good ending, and funny too. Then again . . .

A train pulled up on the downtown side of the track. This was getting tiresome. I was in deeper than I thought. I'd rot in this station waiting for the three train. A nuclear war could come and go, bombs flaring everywhere, and I'd still be waiting here for this dumb number three train!

Finally a three pulled in. I still had my back up against the pole, in case "Spike" came by. When the train stopped, I walked to the first car. The last car is where all the smokers, criminals, and homeless get on, and the front is very close to the conductor.

Wait! I thought, as the doors closed and I found a pole to hold on to. *The middle of the train is the best.* If we got stuck in a tunnel and two trains hit ours from the front and back, only the people in the middle cars would survive. We'd be stuck for hours, even days!

People would turn into cannibals waiting for someone to rescue us. There would be panic. People would be screaming and running all over the place as I sat hunched in a corner eating my Milky Way bar.

"Share it! Share it!" they'd scream, tearing me to shreds and the candy bar too. Eventually they'd let go, after someone grabbed the candy bar from me. Little would they know that I had some M&Ms in my pocket.

Cut! I'm dying here with a bunch of savages even though I'm approaching 96th Street unharmed. The doors opened and a bunch of people got off. I found a seat next to an old lady who probably found it annoying that I continued to pop my gum. She glanced at me. I caught her glance out of the corner of my eye and turned my head. Then all of a sudden she opened her big black pocketbook.

Mace! She had to be pulling out Mace! She'd spray it ruthlessly in my face, then attack me with her cane, again and again, beating me with it until the gum would drop out of my mouth. Then, peacefully, she'd sit back down and read an Our Daily Prayer.

Press the pause button. *C'mon*, I thought. *Would I really get beaten up by an old lady like that?*

"Here, honey. Have something quieter," I heard someone say. It was the old lady. She handed me a sour ball and I thanked her graciously. "Thank you, ma'am, but my parents don't allow me to have candy before dinner. I'll just save this for later."

She looked at me, bewildered. Feeling sorry that I'd been so phony, I spit out my gum, put it back in its wrapper, and put it into my pocket with a whole bunch of other junk. She smiled at me as she got up and stood by the doors; they opened to 125th Street, and she got off.

I began to examine the posters on the overhead walls of the train. Mayor Koch was saying that he wanted me to have his children. A man came around begging for money.

"Please, give what you can. Donate to the poor," he kept saying, walking down the car collecting money in his hat. What if he were to ask me—a kid? Would he ask a kid for money?

"Cough it up in the hat, kid," he'd say. "All kids get their allowance on Thursdays. What do you have? Ten dollars?" Then he'd hang me upside down by my feet, gather up all the change that fell from my pockets, and drop me on my head. I'd lie there unconscious until I found myself in Queens, or maybe the Bronx, or maybe Brooklyn.

Eeeekkk. The train turned and screeched, a horrible sound, like when a kid runs his fingers down a chalkboard. As the train pulled in to its last stop, the conductor instructed people in the back cars to come up front—who knows why?

I stepped off the train and looked at my watch. It was 3:48. I could still make it home in time to watch my television show. I ran inside my building, got the mail, and took the elevator upstairs.

"How was it coming home?" my mom asked as I entered the house.

"Well, it was kinda scary," I said. I mean, meeting "Spike," surviving a nuclear war, daring to be crushed in a train wreck, almost dying for a Milky Way, getting beaten up by an old lady, and almost ending up in Brooklyn, or Queens, or was it the Bronx? . . . is nothing to sneeze at. "But I got over it."

"Good, because you might have to do it again to-morrow."

I swallowed hard, the normal reaction to going home by myself, feeling scared. Then again, it would only be another made-up adventure. But what if . . .

ABOUT THE AUTHOR

Lynya Floyd lives in New York, New York, where she attends The Center School. Besides writing, she enjoys handball (during lunch and after school), computers, television, rock 'n' roll, and spending time with friends.

Story Index
By genre, topic, and for use as writing models